LIFE AND DEATH OF
HARRIETT FREAN

MAY SINCLAIR

LIFE AND DEATH OF HARRIETT FREAN

Introduction by Francine Prose

THE MODERN LIBRARY

NEW YORK

2003 Modern Library Paperback Edition

Introduction copyright © 2003 by Francine Prose
Biographical note and reading group guide copyright © 2003 by
Random House, Inc.

LIBRARY OF CONGRESS CATALOGING-IN-PUBLICATION DATA
Sinclair, May.
Life and death of Harriett Frean/May Sinclair; introduction by Francine Prose.
p. cm.
ISBN 0-8129-6995-2 (trade pbk.)
1. Repression (Psychology)—Fiction. 2. Women—England—Fiction.
3. Single women—Fiction. 4. England—Fiction. I. Title.

PR6037.I73L5   2003
823'.912-dc21   2003051000

Modern Library website address: www.modernlibrary.com

Printed in the United States of America

2   4   6   8   9   7   5   3   1

MAY SINCLAIR

Mary Amelia St. Clair Sinclair was born in Liverpool in 1863. She was the youngest of six children, and the only daughter. When May was seven, her father, an alcoholic shipowner, went bankrupt and left his family. Though her formal education consisted of a single year at the Cheltenham Ladies' College, May Sinclair earned a living writing poetry, translations, criticism, and popular literary fiction. She lived with her mother until Mrs. Sinclair's death in 1901. While she never married, May Sinclair's sparkling circle of literary friends included Thomas Hardy, Henry James, Sarah Orne Jewett, Arnold Bennett, H. G. Wells, John Galsworthy, George Gissing, and Rebecca West.

A member of the Women Writers' Suffrage League and the Women's Freedom League, May Sinclair was a staunch advocate of women's rights. She was also an early champion of the new practice of psychoanalysis, co-founding the Medico-Psychological Clinic and the Tavistock Square Clinic, both in London. During World War I, she briefly served on the Belgian front with an ambulance unit led by the head of the London Medico-Psychological Clinic.

Dubbed England's "leading woman novelist between the death of George Eliot and the rise of Virginia Woolf" by *Punch*, her twenty-nine works of fiction include *The Divine Fire* (1904), *The Three Sisters* (1914), and *The Tree of Heaven* (1917), as well as *Mary Olivier: A Life* (1919) and *Life and Death of Harriett Frean* (1922), two semiautobiographical novels that are noteworthy for incorporating Freudian theory into literature and utilizing stream-of-consciousness writing, a term that Sinclair herself had coined in a review of Dorothy Richardson's novel *Pilgrimage*.

In the late 1920s, May Sinclair began to suffer from Parkinson's disease. She spent the last two decades of her life in a rural nursing home, removed from the public eye. She died on November 14, 1946, in Buckinghamshire, England.

CONTENTS

INTRODUCTION

Francine Prose

For a novel in which there is no physical violence or starvation, in which family members love one another and never raise their voices, in which the characters are, even in the grip of passion, scrupulously polite, *Life and Death of Harriett Frean* nonetheless manages to be one of the more disturbing novels I have read or can imagine.

First published in 1922, May Sinclair's spare, brief book has a deceptively conventional structure—the progress of a woman from birth to death. It tracks the cosseted childhood of its title character, her school years, early friendships and first love, her stunted adulthood, her progressively more circumscribed old age and, at last, her demise. Along the way she suffers the predictable tragic losses that all of us must face: the loss of friends, of love, of parents, of health, of life. But what makes the book so frightening is how few compensations there are, how rare, minor, and misguided the pleasures and satisfactions that might have made it worth Harriett's while to endure the griefs and deprivations.

Harriett Frean is a book that benefits from rereading—if you can bear a second immersion in Harriett's earthly career—for every aspect of the novel has been chosen with great care, and for a purpose. But only when we have grasped the shape of the whole can we return to the early chapters and fully comprehend the compelling reasons for each element's inclusion.

The book begins with a nursery rhyme that baby Harriett loves, a seemingly benign, silly refrain that, in retrospect, comes to sound as portentous as the prophecy of the witches in *Macbeth* or the chanting of a Greek chorus foreshadowing the hero's destiny. It's a familiar bit of doggerel: " 'Pussycat, Pussycat, where have you been?' / 'I've been to London, to see the Queen.' / 'Pussycat, Pussycat, what did you there?' / 'I caught a little mouse under the chair.' " And like Harriett's parents, we're inclined to ask, Why does the baby think it so funny?

Perhaps her infant consciousness is responding to something cautionary or premonitory. Because by the novel's end, the rhyme about the feline who comes to London to do something grand and winds up doing something much smaller (something, in fact, which hardly required leaving home) has become to seem like a parable of the frustration, the distraction, the misperception, and the trivialization of human experience that characterize Harriett's life. Meanwhile, in the opening pages, the rhyme is used to express the comfy, repressed, faintly eroticized connection that the little girl has (and the grown woman will later have) with each of her parents, a bond that will form and sustain and stifle her at once. First Mamma comes into her bedroom and gives her "the kiss-me-to-sleep kiss." Then Papa follows with his "kiss-me-awake kiss."

"Then they played. Papa was the Pussycat and she was the little mouse in her hole under the bed-clothes. They played till Papa said, '*No* more!' and tucked the blankets tight in.

" 'Now you're kissing like Mamma——' "

Soon enough, we begin to appreciate the true cost of all that idyllic, lovey-dovey parent-child affection. Along with their love, Harriett's parents administer, in discreet daily doses, a series of lessons regarding their notions of good behavior, a system that includes not being selfish, not being greedy, not appearing to be greedy, not pushing or shoving, not disobeying. Not betraying the trust of our loved ones. Not being mean, and so forth. When through a misunderstanding Harriett is given (and passively settles for) a plate of crumbs rather than any of the sweet treats being offered at a children's tea, her mother praises her thoroughly unchildlike display of self-abnegation and restraint.

"I'm glad my little girl didn't snatch and push. It's better to go without than to take from other people. That's ugly."

Ugly. Being naughty was just that. Doing ugly things. Being good was being beautiful like Mamma. She wanted to be like her mother....

Suddenly a thought came rushing at her. There was God and there was Jesus. But even God and Jesus were not more beautiful than Mamma.

Harriett is encouraged in this idolatry by her adoring father, the perfect Victorian male, the more-than-perfect Victorian male, a liberal freethinker whose main vice, it seems, is reading Darwin in secret. Eventually, Harriett's father will turn out to be a bit of a self-deluded fraud who bankrupts himself and his hapless neighbor with some sketchy investment advice.

In a few short pages, May Sinclair succeeds in rendering the oppressive weight and strength of the chains of family love, of the craving for parental approval. When Papa gives Harriett this phenomenally mixed message: " 'Forget ugly things. Understand, Hatty, nothing is forbidden. We don't forbid, because we trust you to do what we wish. To behave beautifully.' " Harriett quite naturally concludes that "She would always have to do what they wanted; the unhappiness of not doing it was more than she could bear. All very well to say there would be no punishment; *their* unhappiness was the punishment. It hurt more than anything."

Life and Death of Harriett Frean begins to resemble a nightmare of sorts as it forces its readers to confront the horrifying question: What if you woke up one morning and discovered that you had grown old without progressing much beyond the eager-to-please little girl who did everything her parents wanted? Reading May Sinclair's novel may actually make you feel grateful to live in a time when people talk about things like a young person's need to "separate" from his or her parents. No one offers such advice to Harriett, though there is reason to wish someone had.

When the inevitable crisis occurs—Harriett falls in love with Robin Lethbridge, the fiancé of her frail, pathetic best friend, Priscilla—she much prefers the vision of herself nobly giving up Robin, behaving in the way her parents call "beautiful," to the prospect of a real life with the man she loves. Mourning the loss of the love that this sacrifice has involved, she is comforted only by her parents' reassurance that she has done the right thing.

After Harriett rejects Robin, there is a chapter break, and by the time the novel resumes something dramatic has changed. The author's tone, for one thing. It's as if the authorial eye has pulled back from Harriett and focused on a young woman for whom there is not much chance, a woman destined for a future ruled and determined by upper-middle-class convention, petty snobbery, class consciousness, and self-regard.

Towards spring Harriett showed signs of depression, and they took her to the south of France and to Bordighera and Rome. In Rome she recovered. Rome was one of the places you ought to see; she had always been anxious to do the right thing. In the little Pension in the Via Babuino she had a sense of her own importance and the importance of her father and mother. They were Mr. and Mrs. Hilton Frean, and Miss Harriett Frean, seeing Rome.

On their return, Mr. Frean enjoys an extremely modest literary success as the author of a book entitled *The Social Order*. Harriett and her mother have snappy if stultifying discussions on such topics as whether it is better to read Gibbon first and then see Rome or see Rome and then read Gibbon. Thinking of her lost love, Robin, Harriett feels "a thrill of pleasure in her beautiful behavior, and a thrill of pride in remembering that he had loved her more than Priscilla."

It's a faint pleasure and a thin thrill, as events transpire. Priscilla becomes the victim of a mysterious neurological disorder that transforms the reluctant Robin from a husband into a nursemaid. Within a few years, Harriett's father loses his money—along with that of the unfortunate neighbor's—and promptly sinks into a fatal decline. Harriett's mother dies not long after, while Harriett consoles herself by recalling the most glorious moment of her life—the moment when she gave up Robin for the higher good.

Unfortunately, this moment will turn out to have been more or less pointless, harmful to all concerned, as rife with folly and deception as her father's financial affairs. Indeed, what Harriett discovers when she goes to visit Robin after Priscilla's death makes her heroic and exalted renunciation seem like a senseless joke. When Harriett, against her will, puts together the pieces of what she learns of Robin's life from his second wife, she understands that giving up Robin—a gesture intended to provide a model of nobility and high-mindedness—was in fact a grievous misjudgment that ruined everyone's life. And when Harriett at last accepts the unpleasant truth about who Robin was and who he's become, the most serious damage, we are told, is to Harriett's self-esteem.

From that point on, Harriett's life goes, if it is possible, rather steadily from bad to worse. An appalling household incident (in which Harriett is indirectly involved in the death of a servant's baby) leaves her with little more than "a feeling of insecurity" and reveals her to be ultimately quite heartless. "It rested with Maggie to go or stay," is how she justifies her treatment of her maid. "If she was incompetent I wasn't bound to keep her just because she'd had a baby. At that rate I should have been completely in her power."

There follows an uncomfortable, oddly gratuitous scene in which Robin's young niece informs Harriett—just in case she and the reader haven't figured it out—that her attempt to act beautifully and to save her friend Priscilla's pride was actually "an insult, handing her over to a man who couldn't love her." Robbed of her illusions and lacking enough insight to fill the gaps created by their loss, Harriett descends into a dessicated middle age: "She had no clear illumination, only a mournful acquiescence in her own futility, an almost physical sense of shrinkage, the crumbling away, bit by bit, of her beautiful and honorable self."

In its last section, *Life and Death of Harriett Frean* is Tolstoy's "The Death of Ivan Ilyich" minus the three days of screaming in pain and the predeath revelation that Ivan has lived his whole life wrong. Harriett falls into a "drowsy, supine dependence" on the trusty servant Maggie, the one whose baby died, much as Ivan Ilyich comes to rely on his peasant servant, Gerasim. "She gave up even the semblance of her housekeeping, and became permanently dependent on Maggie. She was happy in the surrender of her responsibility, of the grown-up self she had maintained with so much effort, clinging to Maggie, submitting to Maggie, as she had clung and submitted to her mother."

Finally, Harriett slips away after passing through a stream-of-consciousness fugue state that again evokes the life-wasting Pussycat who went to see the Queen. Harriett's last word, "Mamma," is, as it happens, also her first word in the book—a signal that she has come full circle and basically gone nowhere.

The scariest thing about *Harriett Frean*—and the most courageous aspect of May Sinclair's novel—is that there is little evidence that its protagonist would ever have been a strong or admirable or extraordinary woman were it not for the repressive effects of the moral and social education she gets from her parents. There is no indication that Harriett would ever have been anything but the malleable, shallow, slightly lazy girl who adopts her parents' values rather than go to the trouble of finding her own. She makes a mistake and suffers for it. Nothing works out as planned, there's nothing to make it worthwhile. The little girl desperate to please her parents has grown up and grown old and died.

Such girls are doomed to anxiety. They're always acting, always tap dancing, always checking to see how something is playing with Mamma and Papa. *Life and Death of Harriett Frean* records that terrifying performance enacted, periodically, by certain women, in a culture with only a moderate interest in the fact that there is a difference between women and children. It would be a mistake to assume that lives and deaths like Harriett's ended with the Victorian era or that some modern version of Harriett's life isn't being lived at this moment.

—

FRANCINE PROSE's most recent book is *The Lives of the Muses: Nine Women & the Artists They Inspired*. A contributing editor at *Harper's* and a former director's fellow at the New York Public Library Center for Scholars and Writers, she is the author of ten books of fiction, including *Blue Angel*, a 2000 National Book Award finalist.

LIFE AND DEATH OF
HARRIETT FREAN

I

"Pussycat, Pussycat, where have you been?"
"I've been to London, to see the Queen."
"Pussycat, Pussycat, what did you there?"
"I caught a little mouse under the chair."

Her mother said it three times. And each time the Baby Harriett laughed. The sound of her laugh was so funny that she laughed again at that; she kept on laughing, with shriller and shriller squeals.

"I wonder why she thinks it's funny," her mother said.

Her father considered it. "I don't know. The cat perhaps. The cat and the Queen. But no; that isn't funny."

"She sees something in it we don't see, bless her," said her mother.

Each kissed her in turn, and the Baby Harriett stopped laughing suddenly.

"Mamma, *did* Pussycat see the Queen?"

"No," said Mamma. "Just when the Queen was passing the little mouse came out of its hole and ran under the chair. That's what Pussycat saw."

Every evening before bedtime she said the same rhyme, and Harriett asked the same question.

. . .

When Nurse had gone she would lie still in her cot, waiting. The door would open, the big pointed shadow would move over the ceiling, the lattice shadow of the fireguard would fade and go away, and Mamma would come in carrying the lighted candle. Her face shone white between her long, hanging curls. She would stoop over the cot and lift Harriett up, and her face would be hidden in curls. That was the kiss-me-to-sleep kiss. And when she had gone Harriett lay still again, waiting. Presently Papa would come in, large and dark in the firelight. He stooped and she leapt up into his arms. That was the kiss-me-awake kiss; it was their secret.

Then they played. Papa was the Pussycat and she was the little mouse in her hole under the bed-clothes. They played till Papa said, *"No* more!" and tucked the blankets tight in.

"Now you're kissing like Mamma——"

Hours afterwards they would come again together and stoop over the cot and she wouldn't see them; they would kiss her with soft, light kisses, and she wouldn't know.

She thought: To-night I'll stay awake and see them. But she never did. Only once she dreamed that she heard footsteps and saw the lighted candle, going out of the room; going, going away.

The blue egg stood on the marble top of the cabinet where you could see it from everywhere; it was supported by a gold waistband, by gold hoops and gold legs, and it wore a gold ball with a frill round it like a crown. You would never have guessed what was inside it. You touched a spring in its waistband and it flew open, and then it was a workbox. Gold scissors and thimble and stiletto sitting up in holes cut in white velvet.

The blue egg was the first thing she thought of when she

came into the room. There was nothing like that in Connie Hancock's papa's house. It belonged to Mamma.

Harriett thought: If only she could have a birthday and wake up and find that the blue egg belonged to *her*——

Ida, the wax doll, sat on the drawing-room sofa, dressed ready for the birthday. The darling had real person's eyes made of glass, and real eyelashes and hair. Little finger and toenails were marked in the wax, and she smelt of the lavender her clothes were laid in.

But Emily, the new birthday doll, smelt of composition and of gum and hay; she had flat, painted hair and eyes, and a foolish look on her face, like Nurse's aunt, Mrs. Spinker, when she said "Lawk-a-daisy!" Although Papa had given her Emily, she could never feel for her the real, loving love she felt for Ida.

And her mother had told her that she must lend Ida to Connie Hancock if Connie wanted her.

Mamma couldn't see that such a thing was not possible.

"My darling, you mustn't be selfish. You must do what your little guest wants."

"I can't."

But she had to; and she was sent out of the room because she cried. It was much nicer upstairs in the nursery with Mimi, the Angora cat. Mimi knew that something sorrowful had happened. He sat still, just lifting the root of his tail as you stroked him. If only she could have stayed there with Mimi; but in the end she had to go back to the drawing-room.

If only she could have told Mamma what it felt like to see Connie with Ida in her arms, squeezing her tight to her chest and patting her as if Ida had been *her* child. She kept on saying to herself that Mamma didn't know; she didn't know what she had done. And when it was all over she took the wax doll and put her in the long narrow box she had come in, and buried her in the bottom drawer in the spare-room wardrobe. She thought: If I can't have her to myself I won't have her at all. I've got Emily. I shall just have to pretend she's not an idiot.

She pretended Ida was dead; lying in her paste-board coffin and buried in the wardrobe cemetery.

It was hard work pretending that Emily didn't look like Mrs. Spinker.

II

She had a belief that her father's house was nicer than other people's houses. It stood off from the high road, in Black's Lane, at the head of the town. You came to it by a row of tall elms standing up along Mr. Hancock's wall. Behind the last tree its slender white end went straight up from the pavement, hanging out a green balcony like a birdcage above the green door.

The lane turned sharp there and went on, and the long brown garden wall went with it. Behind the wall the lawn flowed down from the white house and the green veranda to the cedar tree at the bottom. Beyond the lawn was the kitchen garden, and beyond the kitchen garden the orchard; little crippled apple trees bending down in the long grass.

She was glad to come back to the house after the walk with Eliza, the nurse, or Annie, the housemaid; to go through all the rooms looking for Mimi; looking for Mamma, telling her what had happened.

"Mamma, the red-haired woman in the sweetie shop has got a

little baby, and its hair's red, too. . . . Some day I shall have a little baby. I shall dress him in a long gown——"

"Robe."

"Robe, with bands of lace all down it, as long as *that;* and a
white christening cloak sewn with white roses. Won't he look
sweet?"

"Very sweet."

"He shall have lots of hair. I shan't love him if he hasn't."

"Oh, yes, you will."

"No. He must have thick, flossy hair like Mimi, so that I can
stroke him. Which would you rather have, a little girl or a little
boy?"

"Well—what do you think——?"

"I think—perhaps I'd rather have a little girl."

She would be like Mamma, and her little girl would be like
herself. She couldn't think of it any other way.

The school-treat was held in Mr. Hancock's field. All afternoon
she had been with the children, playing Oranges and lemons; A
ring, a ring of roses; and Here we come gathering nuts in May,
nuts in May, *nuts* in May: over and over again. And she had
helped her mother to hand cake and buns at the infants' table.

The guest-children's tea was served last of all, up on the lawn
under the immense, brown brick, many-windowed house. There
wasn't room for everybody at the table, so the girls sat down first
and the boys waited for their turn. Some of them were pushing
and snatching.

She knew what she would have. She would begin with a bun,
and go on through two sorts of jam to Madeira cake, and end
with raspberries and cream. Or perhaps it would be safer to
begin with raspberries and cream. She kept her face very still, so
as not to look greedy, and tried not to stare at the Madeira cake

lest people should see she was thinking of it. Mrs
given her somebody else's crumby plate. She th
greedy. I'm really and truly hungry. She could d
the waist with a flat, exhausted feeling, like the two
concertina coming together.

She was doing this when she saw her mother standing on the
other side of the table, looking at her and making signs.

"If you've finished, Hatty, you'd better get up and let that little boy have something."

They were all turning round and looking at her. And there
was the crumby plate before her. They were thinking: "That
greedy little girl has gone on and on eating." She got up suddenly, not speaking, and left the table, the Madeira cake and the
raspberries and cream. She could feel her skin all hot and wet
with shame.

And now she was sitting up in the drawing-room at home.
Her mother had brought her a piece of seed-cake and a cup of
milk with the cream on it. Mamma's soft eyes kissed her as they
watched her eating her cake with short crumbly bites, like a little cat. Mamma's eyes made her feel so good, so good.

"Why didn't you tell me you hadn't finished?"

"Finished? I hadn't even begun."

"Oh-h, darling, why didn't you *tell* me?"

"Because I—I don't know."

"Well, I'm glad my little girl didn't snatch and push. It's better
to go without than to take from other people. That's ugly."

Ugly. Being naughty was just that. Doing ugly things. Being
good was being beautiful like Mamma. She wanted to be like her
mother. Sitting up there and being good felt delicious. And the
smooth cream with the milk running under it, thin and cold, was
delicious too.

Suddenly a thought came rushing at her. There was God and

...ere was Jesus. But even God and Jesus were not more beautiful than Mamma. They couldn't be.

"You mustn't say things like that, Hatty; you mustn't, really. It might make something happen."

"Oh, no, it won't. You don't suppose they're listening all the time."

Saying things like that made you feel good and at the same time naughty, which was more exciting than only being one or the other. But Mamma's frightened face spoiled it. What did she think—what did she think God would do?

Red campion——

At the bottom of the orchard a door in the wall opened into Black's Lane, below the three tall elms.

She couldn't believe she was really walking there by herself. It had come all of a sudden, the thought that she *must* do it, that she *must* go out into the lane; and when she found the door unlatched, something seemed to take hold of her and push her out. She was forbidden to go into Black's Lane; she was not even allowed to walk there with Annie.

She kept on saying to herself: "I'm in the lane. I'm in the lane. I'm disobeying Mamma."

Nothing could undo that. She had disobeyed by just standing outside the orchard door. Disobedience was such a big and awful thing that it was a waste not to do something big and awful with it. So she went on, up and up, past the three tall elms. She was a big girl, wearing black silk aprons and learning French. Walking by herself. When she arched her back and stuck her stomach out she felt like a tall lady in a crinoline and shawl. She swung her hips and made her skirts fly out. That was her grown-up crinoline, swing-swinging as she went.

At the turn the cow's parsley and rose campion began; on each side a long trail of white froth with the red tops of the campion pricking through. She made herself a nosegay.

Past the second turn you came to the waste ground covered with old boots and rusted, crumpled tins. The little dirty brown house stood there behind the rickety blue palings; narrow, like the piece of a house that has been cut in two. It hid, stooping under the ivy bush on its roof. It was not like the houses people live in; there was something queer, some secret, frightening thing about it.

The man came out and went to the gate and stood there. *He* was the frightening thing. When he saw her he stepped back and crouched behind the palings, ready to jump out.

She turned slowly, as if she had thought of something. She mustn't run. She must *not* run. If she ran he would come after her.

Her mother was coming down the garden walk, tall and beautiful in her silver-gray gown with the bands of black velvet on the flounces and the sleeves; her wide, hooped skirts swung, brushing the flower borders.

She ran up to her, crying, "Mamma, I went up the lane where you told me not to."

"No, Hatty, no; you didn't."

You could see she wasn't angry. She was frightened.

"I did. I did."

Her mother took the bunch of flowers out of her hand and looked at it. "Yes," she said, "that's where the dark-red campion grows."

She was holding the flowers up to her face. It was awful, for you could see her mouth thicken and redden over its edges and shake. She hid it behind the flowers. And somehow you knew it wasn't your naughtiness that made her cry. There was something more.

She was saying in a thick, soft voice, "It was wrong of you, my darling."

Suddenly she bent her tall straightness. "Rose campion," she said, parting the stems with her long, thin fingers. "Look, Hatty, how *beautiful* they are. Run away and put the poor things in water."

She was so quiet, so quiet, and her quietness hurt far more than if she had been angry.

She must have gone straight back into the house to Papa. Harriett knew, because he sent for her. He was quiet, too. . . . That was the little, hiding voice he told you secrets in. . . . She stood close up to him, between his knees, and his arm went loosely round her to keep her there while he looked into her eyes. You could smell tobacco, and the queer, clean man's smell that came up out of him from his collar. He wasn't smiling; but somehow his eyes looked kinder than if they had smiled.

"Why did you do it, Hatty?"

"Because—I wanted to see what it would feel like."

"You mustn't do it again. Do you hear?—you mustn't do it."

"Why?"

"Why? Because it makes your mother unhappy. That's enough why."

But there was something more. Mamma had been frightened. Something to do with the frightening man in the lane.

"Why does it make her?"

She knew; she knew; but she wanted to see what he would say.

"I said that was enough. . . . Do you know what you've been guilty of?"

"Disobedience."

"More than that. Breaking trust. Meanness. It was mean and dishonorable of you when you knew you wouldn't be punished."

"Isn't there to be a punishment?"

"No. People are punished to make them remember. We want you to forget." His arm tightened, drawing her closer. And the kind, secret voice went on. "Forget ugly things. Understand,

Hatty, nothing is forbidden. We don't forbid, because we trust you to do what we wish. To behave beautifully. . . . There, there."

She hid her face on his breast against his tickly coat, and cried.

She would always have to do what they wanted; the unhappiness of not doing it was more than she could bear. All very well to say there would be no punishment; *their* unhappiness was the punishment. It hurt more than anything. It kept on hurting when she thought about it.

The first minute of to-morrow she would begin behaving beautifully; as beautifully as she could. They wanted you to; they wanted it more than anything because they were so beautiful. So good. So wise.

But three years went before Harriett understood how wise they had been, and why her mother took her again and again into Black's Lane to pick red campion, so that it was always the red campion she remembered. They must have known all the time about Black's Lane; Annie, the housemaid, used to say it was a bad place; something had happened to a little girl there. Annie hushed and reddened and wouldn't tell you what it was. Then one day, when she was thirteen, standing by the apple tree, Connie Hancock told her. A secret. . . . Behind the dirty blue palings. . . . She shut her eyes, squeezing the lids down, frightened. But when she thought of the lane she could see nothing but the green banks, the three tall elms, and the red campion pricking through the white froth of the cow's parsley; her mother stood on the garden walk in her wide, swinging gown; she was holding the red and white flowers up to her face and saying, "Look, how *beautiful* they are."

She saw her all the time while Connie was telling her the secret. She wanted to get up and go to her. Connie knew what it meant when you stiffened suddenly and made yourself tall and cold and silent. The cold silence would frighten her and she would go away. Then, Harriett thought, she could get back to her mother and Longfellow.

Every afternoon, through the hours before her father came home, she sat in the cool, green-lighted drawing-room reading *Evangeline* aloud to her mother. When they came to the beautiful places they looked at each other and smiled.

She passed through her fourteenth year sedately, to the sound of *Evangeline*. Her upright body, her lifted, delicately obstinate, rather wistful face expressed her small, conscious determination to be good. She was silent with emotion when Mrs. Hancock told her she was growing like her mother.

III

Connie Hancock was her friend.

She had once been a slender, wide-mouthed child, top-heavy with her damp clumps of hair. Now she was squaring and thickening and looking horrid, like Mr. Hancock. Beside her Harriett felt tall and elegant and slender.

Mamma didn't know what Connie was really like; it was one of those things you couldn't tell her. She said Connie would grow out of it. Meanwhile you could see *he* wouldn't. Mr. Hancock had red whiskers, and his face squatted down in his collar, instead of rising nobly up out of it like Papa's. It looked as if it was thinking things that made its eyes bulge and its mouth curl over and slide like a drawn loop. When you talked about Mr. Hancock, Papa gave a funny laugh as if he was something improper. He said Connie ought to have red whiskers.

Mrs. Hancock, Connie's mother, was Mamma's dearest friend. That was why there had always been Connie. She could remember her, squirming and spluttering in her high nursery chair. And there had always been Mrs. Hancock, refined and mournful, looking at you with gentle, disappointed eyes.

She was glad that Connie hadn't been sent to her boarding-school, so that nothing could come between her and Priscilla Heaven.

Priscilla was her real friend.

It had begun in her third term, when Priscilla first came to the school, unhappy and shy, afraid of the new faces. Harriett took her to her room.

She was thin, thin, in her shabby black velvet jacket. She stood looking at herself in the greenish glass over the yellow-painted chest of drawers. Her heavy black hair had dragged the net and broken it. She put up her thin arms, helpless.

"They'll never keep me," she said. "I'm so untidy."

"It wants more pins," said Harriett. "Ever so many more pins. If you put them in head downwards they'll fall out. I'll show you."

Priscilla trembled with joy when Harriett asked her to walk with her; she had been afraid of her at first because she behaved so beautifully.

Soon they were always together. They sat side by side at the dinner table and in school, black head and golden brown leaning to each other over the same book; they walked side by side in the packed procession, going two by two. They slept in the same room, the two white beds drawn close together; a white dimity curtain hung between; they drew it back so that they could see each other lying there in the summer dusk and in the clear mornings when they waked.

Harriett loved Priscilla's odd, dusk-white face; her long hound's nose, seeking; her wide mouth, restless between her shallow, fragile jaws; her eyes, black, cleared with spots of jade gray, prominent, showing white rims when she was startled. She started at sudden noises; she quivered and stared when you caught her dreaming; she cried when the organ burst out triumphantly in church. You had to take care every minute that you didn't hurt her.

She cried when term ended and she had to go home. Priscilla's home was horrible. Her father drank, her mother fretted; they were poor; a rich aunt paid for her schooling.

When the last midsummer holidays came she spent them with Harriett.

"Oh-h-h!" Prissie drew in her breath when she heard they were to sleep together in the big bed in the spare room. She went about looking at things, curious, touching them softly as if they were sacred. She loved the two rough-coated china lambs on the chimney-piece, and "Oh—the dear little china boxes with the flowers sitting up on them."

But when the bell rang she stood quivering in the doorway.

"I'm afraid of your father and mother, Hatty. They won't like me. I *know* they won't like me."

"They will. They'll love you," Hatty said.

And they did. They were sorry for the little white-faced, palpitating thing.

It was their last night. Priscilla wasn't going back to school again. Her aunt, she said, was only paying for a year. They lay together in the big bed, dim, face to face, talking.

"Hatty—if you wanted to do something most awfully, more than anything else in the world, and it was wrong, would you be able not to do it?"

"I hope so. I *think* I would, because I'd know if I did it would make Papa and Mamma unhappy."

"Yes, but suppose it was giving up something you wanted, something you loved more than them—could you?"

"Yes. If it was wrong for me to have it. And I couldn't love anything more than them."

"But if you did, you'd give it up."

"I'd have to."

"Hatty—I couldn't."

"Oh, yes, *you* could if *I* could."

"No. No. . . ."

"How do you know you couldn't?"

"Because I haven't. I—I oughtn't to have gone on staying here. My father's ill. They wanted me to go to them and I wouldn't go."

"Oh, Prissie——"

"There, you see. But I couldn't. I couldn't. I was so happy here with you. I couldn't give it up."

"If your father had been like Papa you would have."

"Yes. I'd do anything for *him,* because he's your father. It's you I couldn't give up."

"You'll have to some day."

"When—when?"

"When somebody else comes. When you're married."

"I shall never marry. Never. I shall never want anybody but you. If we could always be together. . . . I can't think *why* people marry, Hatty."

"Still," Hatty said, "they do."

"It's because they haven't ever cared as you and me care. . . . Hatty, if I don't marry anybody, *you* won't, will you?"

"I'm not thinking of marrying anybody."

"No. But promise, promise on your honor you won't ever."

"I'd rather not *promise.* You see, I might. I shall love you all the same, Priscilla, all my life."

"No, you won't. It'll all be different. I love you more than you love me. But I shall love you all my life and it won't be different. I shall never marry."

"Perhaps I shan't, either," Harriett said.

They exchanged gifts. Harriett gave Priscilla a rosewood

writing desk inlaid with mother-o'-pearl, and Priscilla gave Harriett a pocket-handkerchief case she had made herself of fine gray canvas embroidered with blue flowers like a sampler and lined with blue and white plaid silk. On the top part you read "Pocket handkerchiefs" in blue lettering, and on the bottom "Harriett Frean," and, tucked away in one corner, "Priscilla Heaven: September, 1861."

IV

She remembered the conversation. Her father sitting, straight and slender, in his chair, talking in that quiet voice of his that never went sharp or deep or quavering, that paused now and then on an amused inflection, his long lips straightening between the perpendicular grooves of his smile. She loved his straight, slender face, clean-shaven, the straight, slightly jutting jaw, the dark-blue flattish eyes under the black eyebrows, the silver-grizzled hair that fitted close like a cap, curling in a silver brim above his ears.

He was talking about his business as if more than anything it amused him.

"There's nothing gross and material about stockbroking. It's like pure mathematics. You're dealing in abstractions, ideal values, all the time. You calculate—in curves." His hand, holding the unlit cigar, drew a curve, a long graceful one, in mid-air. "You know what's going to happen all the time.... The excitement begins when you don't quite know and you risk it; when it's getting dangerous.... The higher mathematics of the game. If you can afford them; if you haven't a wife and family—I can see the fascination...."

He sat holding his cigar in one hand, looking at it without seeing it, seeing the fascination and smiling at it, amused and secure.

And her mother, bending over her bead-work, smiled too, out of their happiness, their security.

He would lean back, smoking his cigar and looking at them out of contented, half-shut eyes, as they stitched, one at each end of the long canvas fender stool. He was waiting, he said, for the moment when their heads would come bumping together in the middle.

Sometimes they would sit like that, not exchanging ideas, exchanging only the sense of each other's presence, a secure, profound satisfaction that belonged as much to their bodies as their minds; it rippled on their faces with their quiet smiling, it breathed with their breath. Sometimes she or her mother read aloud, Mrs. Browning or Charles Dickens; or the biography of some Great Man, sitting there in the velvet-curtained room or out on the lawn under the cedar tree. A motionless communion broken by walks in the sweet-smelling fields and deep, elm-screened lanes. And there were short journeys into London to a lecture or a concert, and now and then the surprise and excitement of the play.

One day her mother smoothed out her long, hanging curls and tucked them away under a net. Harriett had a little shock of dismay and resentment, hating change.

And the long, long Sundays spaced the weeks and the months, hushed and sweet and rather enervating, yet with a sort of thrill in them as if somewhere the music of the church organ went on vibrating. Her mother had some secret: some happy sense of God that she gave to you and you took from her as you took food and clothing, but not quite knowing what it was, feeling that there was something more in it, some hidden gladness, some perfection that you missed.

Her father had his secret too. She felt that it was harder, somehow, darker and dangerous. He read dangerous books: Darwin and Huxley and Herbert Spencer. Sometimes he talked about them.

"There's a sort of fascination in seeing how far you can go.... The fascination of truth might be just that—the risk that, after all, it mayn't be true, that you may have to go farther and farther, perhaps never come back."

Her mother looked up with her bright, still eyes.

"I trust the truth. I know that, however far you go, you'll come back some day."

"I believe you see all of them—Darwin and Huxley and Herbert Spencer—coming back," he said.

"Yes, I do."

His eyes smiled, loving her. But you could see it amused him, too, to think of them, all those reckless, courageous thinkers, coming back, to share her secret. His thinking was just a dangerous game he played.

She looked at her father with a kind of awe as he sat there, reading his book, in danger and yet safe.

She wanted to know what that fascination was. She took down Herbert Spencer and tried to read him. She made a point of finishing every book she had begun, for her pride couldn't bear being beaten. Her head grew hot and heavy: she read the same sentences over and over again; they had no meaning; she couldn't understand a single word of Herbert Spencer. He had beaten her. As she put the book back in its place she said to herself: "I mustn't. If I go on, if I get to the interesting part I may lose my faith." And soon she made herself believe that this was really the reason why she had given it up.

Besides Connie Hancock there were Lizzie Pierce and Sarah Barmby.

Exquisite pleasure to walk with Lizzie Pierce. Lizzie's walk was a sliding, swooping dance of little pointed feet, always as if she were going out to meet somebody, her sharp, black-eyed face darting and turning.

"My *dear,* he kept on doing *this*" (Lizzie did it) "as if he was trying to sit on himself to keep him from flying off into space like a cork. Fancy proposing on three tumblers of soda water! I might have been Mrs. Pennefather but for that."

Lizzie went about laughing, laughing at everybody, looking for something to laugh at everywhere. Now and then she would stop suddenly to contemplate the vision she had created.

"If Connie didn't wear a bustle—or, oh my dear, if Mr. Hancock did——"

"Mr. *Hancock!*" Clear, firm laughter, chiming and tinkling.

"Goodness! To think how many ridiculous people there are in the world!"

"I believe you see something ridiculous in me."

"Only when—only when——"

She swung her parasol in time to her sing-song. She wouldn't say when.

"Lizzie—not—*not* when I'm in my black lace fichu and the little round hat?"

"Oh, dear me—no. Not *then.*"

The little round hat, Lizzie wore one like it herself, tilted forward, perched on her chignon.

"Well, then——" she pleaded.

Lizzie's face darted its teasing, mysterious smile.

She loved Lizzie best of her friends after Priscilla. She loved her mockery and her teasing wit.

And there was Lizzie's friend, Sarah Barmby, who lived in one of those little shabby villas on the London road and looked after her father. She moved about the villa in an unseeing, shambling way, hitting herself against the furniture. Her face was heavy with a gentle, brooding goodness, and she had little eyes that blinked and twinkled in the heaviness, as if something amused her. At first you kept on wondering what the joke was, till you saw it was only a habit Sarah had. She came when she could spare time from her father.

Next to Lizzie, Harriett loved Sarah. She loved her goodness.

And Connie Hancock, bouncing about hospitably in the large, rich house. Tea-parties and dances at the Hancocks'.

She wasn't sure that she liked dancing. There was something obscurely dangerous about it. She was afraid of being lifted off her feet and swung on and on, away from her safe, happy life. She was stiff and abrupt with her partners, convinced that none of those men who liked Connie Hancock could like her, and anxious to show them that she didn't expect them to. She was afraid of what they were thinking. And she would slip away early, running down the garden to the gate at the bottom of the lane where her father waited for her. She loved the still coldness of the night under the elms, and the strong, tight feel of her father's arm when she hung on it leaning towards him, and his "There we are!" as he drew her closer. Her mother would look up from the sofa and ask always the same question, "Well, did anything nice happen?"

Till at last she answered, "No. Did you think it would, Mamma?"

"You never know," said her mother.

"*I* know everything."

"*Every*thing?"

"Everything that could happen at the Hancocks' dances."

Her mother shook her head at her. She knew that in secret Mamma was glad; but she answered the reproof.

"It's mean of me to say that when I've eaten four of their ices. They were strawberry, and chocolate and vanilla, all in one."

"Well, they won't last much longer."

"Not at that rate," her father said.

"I meant the dances," said her mother.

And sure enough, soon after Connie's engagement to young Mr. Pennefather, they ceased.

And the three friends, Connie and Sarah and Lizzie, came and went. She loved them; and yet when they were there they broke something, something secret and precious between her and her father and mother, and when they were gone she felt the stir, the happy movement of coming together again, drawing in close, close, after the break.

"We only want each other." Nobody else really mattered, not even Priscilla Heaven.

Year after year the same. Her mother parted her hair into two sleek wings; she wore a rosette and lappets of black velvet and lace on a glistening beetle-backed chignon. And Harriett felt again her shock of resentment. She hated to think of her mother subject to change and time.

And Priscilla came year after year, still loving, still protesting that she would never marry. Yet they were glad when even Priscilla had gone and left them to each other. Only each other, year after year the same.

V

Priscilla's last visit was followed by another passionate vow that she would never marry. Then within three weeks she wrote again, telling of her engagement to Robin Lethbridge.

"... I haven't known him very long, and Mamma says it's too soon; but he makes me feel as if I had known him all my life. I know I said I wouldn't, but I couldn't tell; I didn't know it would be so different. I couldn't have believed that anybody could be so happy. You won't mind, Hatty. We can love each other just the same...."

Incredible that Priscilla, who could be so beaten down and crushed by suffering, should have risen to such an ecstasy. Her letters had a swinging lilt, a hurried beat, like a song bursting, a heart beating for joy too fast.

It would have to be a long engagement. Robin was in a provincial bank, he had his way to make. Then, a year later, Prissy wrote and told them that Robin had got a post in Parson's Bank in the City. He didn't know a soul in London. Would they be kind to him and let him come to them sometimes, on Saturdays and Sundays?

He came one Sunday. Harriett had wondered what he would be like, and he was tall, slender-waisted, wide-shouldered; he had a square, very white forehead; his brown hair was parted on one side, half curling at the tips above his ears. His eyes—thin, black crystal, shining, turning, showing speckles of brown and gray; perfectly set under straight eyebrows laid very black on the white skin. His round, pouting chin had a dent in it. The face in between was thin and irregular; the nose straight and serious and rather long in profile, with a dip and a rise at three-quarters; in full face straight again but shortened. His eyes had another meaning, deeper and steadier than his fine slender mouth; but it was the mouth that made you look at him. One arch of the bow was higher than the other; now and then it quivered with an uneven, sensitive movement of its own.

She noticed his mouth's little dragging droop at the corners and thought: "Oh, you're cross. If you're cross with Prissie—if you make her unhappy"—but when he caught her looking at him the cross lips drew back in a sudden, white, confiding smile. And when he spoke she understood why he had been irresistible to Priscilla.

He had come three Sundays now, four perhaps; she had lost count. They were all sitting out on the lawn under the cedar. Suddenly, as if he had only just thought of it, he said:

"It's extraordinarily good of you to have me."

"Oh, well," her mother said, "Prissie is Hatty's greatest friend."

"I supposed that was why you do it."

He didn't want it to be that. He wanted it to be himself. Himself. He was proud. He didn't like to owe anything to other people, not even to Prissie.

Her father smiled at him. "You must give us time."

He would never give it or take it. You could see him tearing at things in his impatience, to know them, to make them give themselves up to him at once. He came rushing to give himself up, all in a minute, to make himself known.

"It isn't fair," he said. "I know you so much better than you know me. Priscilla's always talking about you. But you don't know anything about *me.*"

"No. We've got all the excitement."

"And the risk, sir."

"And, of course, the risk." He liked him.

She could talk to Robin Lethbridge as she couldn't talk to Connie Hancock's young men. She wasn't afraid of what he was thinking. She was safe with him, he belonged to Priscilla Heaven. He liked her because he loved Priscilla; but he wanted her to like him, not because of Priscilla, but for himself.

She talked about Priscilla: "I never saw anybody so loving. It used to frighten me; because you can hurt her so easily."

"Yes. Poor little Prissie, she's very vulnerable," he said.

When Priscilla came to stay it was almost painful. Her eyes clung to him, and wouldn't let him go. If he left the room she was restless, unhappy till he came back. She went out for long walks with him and returned silent, with a tired, beaten look. She would lie on the sofa, and he would hang over her, gazing at her with strained, unhappy eyes.

After she had gone he kept on coming more than ever, and he stayed overnight. Harriett had to walk with him now. He wanted to talk, to talk about himself, endlessly.

When she looked in the glass she saw a face she didn't know: bright-eyed, flushed, pretty. The little arrogant lift had gone. As if it had been somebody else's face she asked herself, in wonder, without rancor, why nobody had ever cared for it. Why? Why? She could see her father looking at her, intent, as if he wondered. And one day her mother said, "Do you think you ought to see so much of Robin? Do you think it's quite fair to Prissie?"

"Oh—*Mamma!* . . . I wouldn't. I haven't——"

"I know. You couldn't if you would, Hatty. You would always behave beautifully. But are you so sure about Robin?"

"Oh, he *couldn't* care for *anybody* but Prissie. It's only because he's so safe with me, because he knows I don't and he doesn't——"

The wedding day was fixed for July. After all, they were going to risk it. By the middle of June the wedding presents began to come in.

Harriett and Robin Lethbridge were walking up Black's Lane. The hedges were a white bridal froth of cow's parsley. Every now and then she swerved aside to pick the red campion.

He spoke suddenly. "Do you know what a dear little face you have, Hatty? It's so clear and still and it behaves so beautifully."

"Does it?"

She thought of Prissie's face, dark and restless, never clear, never still.

"You're not a bit like what I expected. Prissie doesn't know what you are. You don't know yourself."

"I know what *she* is."

His mouth's uneven quiver beat in and out like a pulse.

"Don't talk to me about Prissie!"

Then he got it out. He tore it out of himself. He loved her.

"Oh, Robin——" Her fingers loosened in her dismay; she went dropping red campion.

It was no use, he said, to think about Prissie. He couldn't marry her. He couldn't marry anybody but Hatty; Hatty must marry him.

"You can't say you don't love me, Hatty."

No. She couldn't say it; for it wouldn't be true.

"Well, then——"

"I can't. I'd be doing wrong, Robin. I feel all the time as if she belonged to you; as if she were married to you."

"But she isn't. It isn't the same thing."

"To me it is. You can't undo it. It would be too dishonorable."

"Not half so dishonorable as marrying her when I don't love her."

"Yes. As long as she loves you. She hasn't anybody but you. She was so happy. So happy. Think of the cruelty of it. Think what we should send her back to."

"You think of Prissie. You don't think of me."

"Because it would *kill* her."

"How about you?"

"It can't kill us, because we know we love each other. Nothing can take that from us."

"But I couldn't be happy with her, Hatty. She wears me out. She's so restless."

"*We* couldn't be happy, Robin. We should always be thinking of what we did to her. How could we be happy?"

"You know how."

"Well, even if we were, we've no right to get our happiness out of her suffering."

"Oh, Hatty, why are you so good, so good?"

"I'm not good. It's only—there are some things you can't do. We couldn't. We couldn't."

"No," he said at last. "I don't suppose we could. Whatever it's like I've got to go through with it."

He didn't stay that night.

She was crouching on the floor beside her father, her arm thrown across his knees. Her mother had left them there.

"Papa—do you know?"

"Your mother told me. . . . You've done the right thing."

"You don't think I've been cruel? He said I didn't think of him."

"Oh, no, you couldn't do anything else."

She couldn't. She couldn't. It was no use thinking about him. Yet night after night, for weeks and months, she thought, and cried herself to sleep.

By day she suffered from Lizzie's sharp eyes and Sarah's brooding pity and Connie Pennefather's callous, married stare. Only with her father and mother she had peace.

VI

Towards spring Harriett showed signs of depression, and they took her to the south of France and to Bordighera and Rome. In Rome she recovered. Rome was one of those places you ought to see; she had always been anxious to do the right thing. In the little Pension in the Via Babuino she had a sense of her own importance and the importance of her father and mother. They were Mr. and Mrs. Hilton Frean, and Miss Harriett Frean, seeing Rome.

After their return in the summer he began to write his book, *The Social Order.* There were things that had to be said; it did not much matter who said them provided they were said plainly. He dreamed of a new Social State, society governing itself without representatives. For a long time they lived on the interest and excitement of the book, and when it came out Harriett pasted all his reviews very neatly into an album. He had the air of not taking them quite seriously; but he subscribed to *The Spectator,* and sometimes an article appeared there understood to have been written by Hilton Frean.

And they went abroad again every year. They went to Florence and came home and read *Romola* and Mrs. Browning and Dante and *The Spectator;* they went to Assisi and read the *Little Flowers of Saint Francis;* they went to Venice and read Ruskin and *The Spectator;* they went to Rome again and read Gibbon's *Decline and Fall of the Roman Empire.* Harriett said, "We should have enjoyed Rome more if we had read Gibbon," and her mother replied that they would not have enjoyed Gibbon so much if they had not seen Rome. Harriett did not really enjoy him; but she enjoyed the sound of her own voice reading out the great sentences and the rolling Latin names.

She had brought back photographs of the Colosseum and the Forum and of Botticelli's *Spring,* and a della Robbia Madonna in a shrine of fruit and flowers, and hung them in the drawing-room. And when she saw the blue egg in its gilt frame standing on the marble-topped table, she wondered how she had ever loved it, and wished it were not there. It had been one of Mamma's wedding presents. Mrs. Hancock had given it her; but Mr. Hancock must have bought it.

Harriett's face had taken on again its arrogant lift. She esteemed herself justly. She knew she was superior to the Hancocks and the Pennefathers and to Lizzie Pierce and Sarah Barmby; even to Priscilla. When she thought of Robin and how she had given him up she felt a thrill of pleasure in her beautiful behavior, and a thrill of pride in remembering that he had loved her more than Priscilla. Her mind refused to think of Robin married.

Two, three, five years passed, with a perceptible acceleration, and Harriett was now thirty.

She had not seen them since the wedding day. Robin had gone back to his own town; he was cashier in a big bank there. For four years Prissie's letters came regularly every month or so, then ceased abruptly.

Then Robin wrote and told her of Prissie's illness. A mysterious paralysis. It had begun with fits of giddiness in the street; Prissie would turn round and round on the pavement; then falling fits; and now both legs were paralyzed, but Robin thought she was gradually recovering the use of her hands.

Harriett did not cry. The shock of it stopped her tears. She tried to see it and couldn't. Poor little Prissie. How terrible. She kept on saying to herself she couldn't bear to think of Prissie paralyzed. Poor little Prissie.

And poor Robin——

Paralysis. She saw the paralysis coming between them, separating them, and inside her the secret pain was soothed. She need not think of Robin married any more.

She was going to stay with them. Robin had written the letter. He said Prissie wanted her. When she met him on the platform she had a little shock at seeing him changed. Changed. His face was fuller, and a dark mustache hid the sensitive, uneven, pulsing lip. His mouth was dragged down further at the corners. But he was the same Robin. In the cab, going to the house, he sat silent, breathing hard; she felt the tremor of his consciousness and knew that he still loved her; more than he loved Priscilla. Poor little Prissie. How terrible!

Priscilla sat by the fireplace in a wheel chair. She became agitated when she saw Harriett; her arms shook as she lifted them for the embrace.

"Hatty—you've hardly changed a bit." Her voice shook.

Poor little Prissie. She was thin, thinner than ever, and stiff as if she had withered. Her face was sallow and dry, and the luster had gone from her black hair. Her wide mouth twitched and wavered, wavered and twitched. Though it was warm summer she sat by a blazing fire with the windows behind her shut.

Through dinner Harriett and Robin were silent and con-
strained. She tried not to see Prissie shaking and jerking and
spilling soup down the front of her gown. Robin's face was
smooth and blank; he pretended to be absorbed in his food, so as
not to look at Prissie. It was as if Prissie's old restlessness had
grown into that ceaseless jerking and twitching. And her eyes
fastened on Robin; they clung to him and wouldn't let him go.
She kept on asking him to do things for her. "Robin, you might
get me my shawl;" and Robin would go and get the shawl and put
it round her. Whenever he did anything for her Prissie's face
would settle down into a quivering, deep content.

At nine o'clock he lifted her out of her wheel chair. Harriett
saw his stoop, and the taut, braced power of his back as he lifted.
Prissie lay in his arms with rigid limbs hanging from loose at-
tachments, inert, like a doll. As he carried her upstairs to bed her
face had a queer, exalted look of pleasure and of triumph.

Harriett and Robin sat alone together in his study.

"How long is it since we've seen each other?"

"Five years, Robin."

"It isn't. It can't be."

"It is."

"I suppose it is. But I can't believe it. I can't believe I'm married. I can't believe Prissie's ill. It doesn't seem real with you sitting there."

"Nothing's changed, Robin, except that you're more serious."

"Nothing's changed, except that I'm more serious than ever.
. . . Do you still do the same things? Do you still sit in the curly
chair, holding your work up to your chin with your little pointed
hands like a squirrel? Do you still see the same people?"

"I don't make new friends, Robin."

He seemed to settle down after that, smiling at his own
thoughts, appeased . . .

Lying in her bed in the spare room, Harriett heard the opening and shutting of Robin's door. She still thought of Prissie's paralysis as separating them, still felt inside her a secret, unacknowledged satisfaction. Poor little Prissie. How terrible. Her pity for Priscilla went through and through her in wave after wave. Her pity was sad and beautiful and at the same time it appeased her pain.

In the morning Priscilla told her about her illness. The doctors didn't understand it. She ought to have had a stroke and she hadn't had one. There was no reason why she shouldn't walk except that she couldn't. It seemed to give her pleasure to go over it, from her first turning round and round in the street (with helpless, shaking laughter at the queerness of it), to the moment when Robin bought her the wheel chair. . . . Robin . . . Robin . . . "I minded most because of Robin. It's such an *awful* illness, Hatty. I can't move when I'm in bed. Robin has to get up and turn me a dozen times in one night. . . . Robin's a perfect saint. He does everything for me." Prissie's voice and her face softened and thickened with voluptuous content.

". . . Do you know, Hatty, I had a little baby. It died the day it was born. . . . Perhaps some day I shall have another."

Harriett was aware of a sudden tightening of her heart, of a creeping depression that weighed on her brain and worried it. She thought this was her pity for Priscilla.

Her third night. All evening Robin had been moody and morose. He would hardly speak to either Harriett or Priscilla. When Priscilla asked him to do anything for her he got up heavily, pulling himself together with a sigh, with a look of weary, irritated patience.

Prissie wheeled herself out of the study into the drawing-room, beckoning Harriett to follow. She had the air of saving

Robin from Harriett, of intimating that his grumpiness was Harriett's fault. "He doesn't want to be bothered," she said.

She sat up till eleven, so that Robin shouldn't be thrown with Harriett in the last hours.

Half the night Harriett's thoughts ran on, now in a darkness, now in thin flashes of light. "Supposing, after all, Robin wasn't happy? Supposing he can't stand it? Supposing. . . . But why is he angry with *me?*" Then a clear thought: "He's angry with me because he can't be angry with Priscilla." And clearer. "He's angry with me because I made him marry her."

She stopped the running and meditated with a steady, hard deliberation. She thought of her deep, spiritual love for Robin; of Robin's deep spiritual love for her; of his strength in shouldering his burden. It was through her renunciation that he had grown so strong, so pure, so good.

Something had gone wrong with Prissie. Robin, coming home early on Saturday afternoon, had taken Harriett for a walk. All evening and all through Sunday it was Priscilla who sulked and snapped when Harriett spoke to her.

On Monday morning she was ill, and Robin ordered her to stay in bed. Monday was Harriett's last night. Priscilla stayed in bed till six o'clock, when she heard Robin come in; then she insisted on being dressed and carried downstairs. Harriett heard her calling to Robin, and Robin saying, "I *told* you you weren't to get up till to-morrow," and a sound like Prissie crying.

At dinner she shook and jerked and spilt things worse than ever. Robin gloomed at her. "You know you ought to be in bed. You'll go at nine."

"If I go, you'll go. You've got a headache."

"I should think I had, sitting in this furnace."

The heat of the dining room oppressed him, but they sat on

there after dinner because Prissie loved the heat. Robin's pale, blank face had a sick look, a deadly smoothness. He had to lie down on the sofa in the window.

When the clock struck nine he sighed and got up, dragging himself as if the weight of his body was more than he could bear. He stooped over Prissie, and lifted her.

"Robin—you can't. You're dropping to pieces."

"I'm all right." He heaved her up with one tremendous, irritated effort, and carried her upstairs, fast, as if he wanted to be done with it. Through the open doors Harriett could hear Prissie's pleading whine, and Robin's voice, hard and controlled. Presently he came back to her and they went into his study. They could breathe there, he said.

They sat without speaking for a little time. The silence of Prissie's room overhead came between them.

Robin spoke first. "I'm afraid it hasn't been very gay for you with poor Prissie in this state."

"Poor Prissie? She's very happy, Robin."

He stared at her. His eyes, round and full and steady, taxed her with falsehood, with hypocrisy.

"You don't suppose *I'm* not, do you?"

"No." There was a movement in her throat as though she swallowed something hard. "No. I want you to be happy."

"You don't. You want me to be rather miserable."

"Robin!" She contrived a sound like laughter. But Robin didn't laugh; his eyes, morose and cynical, held her there.

"That's what you want. . . . At least I hope you do. If you didn't——"

She fenced off the danger. "Do *you* want *me* to be miserable, then?"

At that he laughed out. "No. I don't. I don't care how happy you are."

She took the pain of it: the pain he meant to give her.

That evening he hung over Priscilla with a deliberate, exaggerated tenderness.

"Dear.... Dearest...." He spoke the words to Priscilla, but he sent out his voice to Harriett. She could feel its false precision, its intention, its repulse of her.

She was glad to be gone.

VII

Eighteen Seventy-nine: it was the year her father lost his money. Harriett was nearly thirty-five.

She remembered the day, late in November, when they heard him coming home from the office early. Her mother raised her head and said, "That's your father, Harriett. He must be ill." She always thought of seventy-nine as one continuous November.

Her father and mother were alone in the study for a long time; she remembered Annie going in with the lamp and coming out and whispering that they wanted her. She found them sitting in the lamplight alone, close together, holding each other's hands; their faces had a strange, exalted look.

"Harriett, my dear, I've lost every shilling I possessed, and here's your mother saying she doesn't mind."

He began to explain in his quiet voice. "When all the creditors are paid in full there'll be nothing but your mother's two hundred a year. And the insurance money when I'm gone."

"Oh, Papa, how terrible——"

"Yes, Hatty."

"I mean the insurance. It's gambling with your life."

"My dear, if that was all I'd gambled with——"

It seemed that half his capital had gone in what he called "the higher mathematics of the game." The creditors would get the rest.

"We shall be no worse off," her mother said, "than we were when we began. We were very happy then."

"We. How about Harriett?"

"Harriett isn't going to mind."

"You're not—going—to mind. . . . We shall have to sell this house and live in a smaller one. And I can't take my business up again."

"My dear, I'm glad and thankful you've done with that dreadful, dangerous game."

"I'd no business to play it. . . . But, after holding myself in all those years, there was a sort of fascination."

One of the creditors, Mr. Hichens, gave him work in his office. He was now Mr. Hichens's clerk. He went to Mr. Hichens as he had gone to his own great business, upright and alert, handsome in his dark-gray overcoat with the black velvet collar, faintly amused at himself. You would never have known that anything had happened.

Strange that at the same time Mr. Hancock should have lost money, a great deal of money, more money than Papa. He seemed determined that everybody should know it; you couldn't pass him in the road without knowing. He met you with his swollen, red face hanging; ashamed and miserable, and angry as if it had been your fault.

One day Harriett came in to her father and mother with the news. "Did you know that Mr. Hancock's sold his horses? And he's going to give up the house."

Her mother signed to her to be silent, frowning and shaking her head and glancing at her father. He got up suddenly and left the room.

"He's worrying himself to death about Mr. Hancock," she said.

"I didn't know he cared for him like that, Mamma."

"Oh, well, he's known him thirty years, and it's a very dreadful thing he should have to give up his house."

"It's not worse for him than it is for Papa."

"It's ever so much worse. He isn't like your father. He can't be happy without his big house and his carriages and horses. He'll feel so small and unimportant."

"Well, then, it serves him right."

"Don't say that. It *is* what he cares for and he's lost it."

"He's no business to behave as if it was Papa's fault," said Harriett. She had no patience with the odious little man. She thought of her father's face, her father's body, straight and calm, and his soul so far above that mean trouble of Mr. Hancock's, that vulgar shame.

Yet inside him he fretted. And, suddenly, he began to sink. He turned faint after the least exertion and had to leave off going to Mr. Hichens. And by the spring of eighteen eighty he was upstairs in his room, too ill to be moved. That was just after Mr. Hichens had bought the house and wanted to come into it. He lay, patient, in the big white bed, smiling his faint, amused smile when he thought of Mr. Hichens.

It was awful to Harriett that her father should be ill, lying there at their mercy. She couldn't get over her sense of his parenthood, his authority. When he was obstinate, and insisted on exerting himself, she gave in. She was a bad nurse, because she couldn't set herself against his will. And when she had him under her hands to strip and wash him, she felt that she was doing something outrageous and impious; she set about it with a flaming face and fumbling hands. "Your mother does it better," he said gently. But she could not get her mother's feeling of him as a helpless, dependent thing.

Mr. Hichens called every week to inquire. "Poor man, he wants to know when he can have his house. Why *will* he always come on my good days? He isn't giving himself a chance."

He still had good days, days when he could be helped out of bed to sit in his chair. "This sort of game may go on for ever," he said. He began to worry seriously about keeping Mr. Hichens out of his house. "It isn't decent of me. It isn't decent."

Harriett was ill with the strain of it. She had to go away for a fortnight with Lizzie Pierce, and Sarah Barmby stayed with her mother. Mrs. Barmby had died the year before. When Harriett got back her father was making plans for his removal.

"Why have you all made up your minds that it'll kill me to remove me? It won't. The men can take everything out but me and my bed and that chair. And when they've got all the things into the other house they can come back for the chair and me. And I can sit in the chair while they're bringing the bed. It's quite simple. It only wants a little system."

Then, while they wondered whether they might risk it, he got worse. He lay propped up, rigid, his arms stretched out by his side, afraid to lift a hand because of the violent movements of his heart. His face had a patient, expectant look, as if he waited for them to do something.

They couldn't do anything. There would be no more rallies. He might die any day now, the doctor said.

"He may die any minute. I certainly don't expect him to live through the night."

Harriett followed her mother back into the room. He was sitting up in his attitude of rigid expectancy; no movement but the quivering of his night-shirt above his heart.

"The doctor's been gone a long time, hasn't he?" he said.

Harriett was silent. She didn't understand. Her mother was looking at her with a serene comprehension and compassion.

"Poor Hatty," he said, "she can't tell a lie to save my life."

"Oh—Papa——"

He smiled as if he was thinking of something that amused him.

"You should consider other people, my dear. Not just your own selfish feelings. . . . You ought to write and tell Mr. Hichens."

Her mother gave a short sobbing laugh. "Oh, you darling," she said.

He lay still. Then suddenly he began pressing hard on the mattress with both hands, bracing himself up in the bed. Her mother leaned closer towards him. He threw himself over slant-ways, and with his head bent as if it was broken, dropped into her arms.

Harriett wondered why he was making that queer grating and coughing noise. Three times.

Her mother called softly to her—"Harriett."

She began to tremble.

VIII

Her mother had some secret that she couldn't share. She was wonderful in her pure, high serenity. Surely she had some secret. She said he was closer to her now than he had ever been. And in her correct, precise answers to the letters of condolence Harriett wrote: "I feel that he is closer to us now than he ever was." But she didn't really feel it. She only felt that to feel it was the beautiful and proper thing. She looked for her mother's secret and couldn't find it.

Meanwhile Mr. Hichens had given them six weeks. They had to decide where they would go: into Devonshire or into a cottage at Hampstead where Sarah Barmby lived now.

Her mother said, "Do you think you'd like to live in Sidmouth, near Aunt Harriett?"

They had stayed one summer at Sidmouth with Aunt Harriett. She remembered the red cliffs, the sea, and Aunt Harriett's garden stuffed with flowers. They had been happy there. She thought she would love that: the sea and the red cliffs and a garden like Aunt Harriett's.

But she was not sure whether it was what her mother really wanted. Mamma would never say. She would have to find out somehow.

"Well—what do you think?"

"It would be leaving all your friends, Hatty."

"My friends—yes. But——"

Lizzie and Sarah and Connie Pennefather. She could live without them. "Oh, there's Mrs. Hancock."

"Well——" Her mother's voice suggested that if she were put to it she could live without Mrs. Hancock.

And Harriett thought: She does want to go to Sidmouth then.

"It would be very nice to be near Aunt Harriett."

She was afraid to say more than that lest she should show her own wish before she knew her mother's.

"Aunt Harriett. Yes. . . . But it's very far away, Hatty. We should be cut off from everything. Lectures and concerts. We couldn't afford to come up and down."

"No. We couldn't."

She could see that Mamma did not really want to live in Sidmouth; she didn't want to be near Aunt Harriett; she wanted the cottage at Hampstead and all the things of their familiar, intellectual life going on and on. After all, that was the way to keep near to Papa, to go on doing the things they had done together.

Her mother agreed that it was the way.

"I can't help feeling," Harriett said, "it's what he would have wished."

Her mother's face was quiet and content. She hadn't guessed.

They left the white house with the green balcony hung out like a birdcage at the side, and turned into the cottage at Hampstead. The rooms were small and rather dark, and the furniture they had brought had a squeezed-up, unhappy look. The blue egg on the marble-topped table was conspicuous and hateful as it had never been in the Black's Lane drawing-room. Harriett and her mother looked at it.

"Must it stay there?"

"I think so. Fanny Hancock gave it me."

"Mamma—you know you don't like it."

"No. But after all these years I couldn't turn the poor thing away."

Her mother was an old woman, clinging with an old, stubborn fidelity to the little things of her past. But Harriett denied it. "She's not old," she said to herself. "Not really old."

"Harriett," her mother said one day. "I think you ought to do the housekeeping."

"Oh, Mamma, why?" She hated the idea of this change.

"Because you'll have to do it some day."

She obeyed. But as she went her rounds and gave her orders she felt that she was doing something not quite real, playing at being her mother as she had played when she was a child. Then her mother had another thought.

"Harriett, I think you ought to see more of your friends, dear."

"Why?"

"Because you'll want them after I'm gone."

"I shall never *want* anybody but you."

And their time went as it had gone before: in sewing together, reading together, listening to lectures and concerts together. They had told Sarah that they didn't want anybody to call. They were Hilton Frean's wife and daughter. "After our wonderful life with him," they said, "you'll understand, Sarah, that we don't want people." And if Harriett was introduced to any stranger she accounted for herself arrogantly: "My father was Hilton Frean."

They were collecting his *Remains* for publication.

Months passed, years passed, going each one a little quicker than the last. And Harriett was thirty-nine.

One evening, coming out of church, her mother fainted. That was the beginning of her illness, February, eighteen eighty-three. First came the long months of weakness; then the months and months of sickness; then the pain; the pain she had been hiding, that she couldn't hide any more.

They knew what it was now: that horrible thing that even the doctors were afraid to name. They called it "something malignant." When the friends—Mrs. Hancock, Connie Pennefather, Lizzie, and Sarah—called to inquire, Harriett wouldn't tell them what it was; she pretended that she didn't know, that the doctors weren't sure; she covered it up from them as if it had been a secret shame. And they pretended that they didn't know. But they knew.

They were talking now about an operation. There was one chance for her in a hundred if they had Sir James Pargeter: one chance. She might die of it; she might die under the anæsthetic; she might die of shock; she was so old and weak. Still, there was that one chance, if only she would take it.

But her mother wouldn't listen. "My dear, it would cost a hundred pounds."

"How do you know what it would cost?"

"Oh," she said, "I know." She was smiling above the sheet that was tucked close up, tight under her chin, shutting it all down.

Sir James Pargeter would cost a hundred pounds. Harriett couldn't lay her hands on the money or on half of it or a quarter. "That doesn't matter if they think it'll save you."

"They *think*; they think. But I *know*. I know better than all the doctors."

"But Mamma, darling——"

She urged the operation. Just because it would be so difficult to raise the hundred pounds she urged it. She wanted to feel that she had done everything that could be done, that she had let nothing stand in the way, that she had shrunk from no sacrifice. One chance in a hundred. What was a hundred pounds weighed against that one chance? If it had been one in a thousand she would have said the same.

"It would be no good, Hatty. I know it wouldn't. They just love to try experiments, those doctors. They're dying to get their knives into me. Don't *let* them."

Gradually, day by day, Harriett weakened. Her mother's frightened voice tore at her, broke her down. Supposing she really died under the operation? Supposing—— It was cruel to excite and upset her just for that; it made the pain worse.

Either the operation or the pain, going on and on, stabbing with sharper and sharper knives; cutting in deeper; all their care, the antiseptics, the restoratives, dragging it out, giving it more time to torture her.

When the three friends came, Harriett said, "I shall be glad and thankful when it's all over. I couldn't want to keep her with me, just for this."

Yet she did want it. She was thankful every morning that she came to her mother's bed and found her alive, lying there, looking at her with her wonderful smile. She was glad because she still had her.

And now they were giving her morphia. Under the torpor of the drug her face changed; the muscles loosened, the flesh sagged, the widened, swollen mouth hung open; only the broad beautiful forehead, the beautiful calm eyebrows were the same; the face, sallow white, half imbecile, was a mask flung aside. She couldn't bear to look at it; it wasn't her mother's face; her mother had died already under the morphia. She had a shock every time she came in and found it still there.

On the day her mother died she told herself she was glad and thankful. She met her friends with a little quiet, composed face, saying, "I'm glad and thankful she's at peace." But she wasn't thankful; she wasn't glad. She wanted her back again. And she reproached herself, one minute for having been glad, and the next for wanting her.

She consoled herself by thinking of the sacrifices she had made, how she had given up Sidmouth, and how willingly she would have paid the hundred pounds.

"I sometimes think, Hatty," said Mrs. Hancock, melancholy and condoling, "that it would have been very different if your poor mother could have had her wish."

"What—what wish?"

"Her wish to live in Sidmouth, near your Aunt Harriett."

And Sarah Barmby, sympathizing heavily, stopping short and brooding, trying to think of something to say: "If the operation had only been done three years ago when they *knew* it would save her——"

"Three years ago? But we didn't know anything about it then."

"*She* did. . . . Don't you remember? It was when I stayed with her. . . . Oh, Hatty, didn't she tell you?"

"She never said a word."

"Oh, well, she wouldn't hear of it, even then when they didn't give her two years to live."

Three years? She had had it three years ago. She had known about it all that time. Three years ago the operation would have saved her; she would have been here now. Why had she refused it when she knew it would save her?

She had been thinking of the hundred pounds.

To have known about it three years and said nothing—to have gone believing she hadn't two years to live——

That was her secret. That was why she had been so calm when Papa died. She had known she would have him again so soon. Not two years——

"If I'd been them," Lizzie was saying, "I'd have bitten my tongue out before I told you. It's no use worrying, Hatty. You did everything that could be done."

"I know. I know."

She held up her face against them; but to herself she said that everything had not been done. Her mother had never had her wish. And she had died in agony, so that she, Harriett, might keep her hundred pounds.

IX

In all her previsions of the event she had seen herself surviving as the same Harriett Frean with the addition of an overwhelming grief. She was horrified at this image of herself persisting beside her mother's place empty in space and time.

But she was not there. Through her absorption in her mother, some large, essential part of herself had gone. It had not been so when her father died; what he had absorbed was given back to her, transferred to her mother. All her memories of her mother were joined to the memory of this now irrecoverable self.

She tried to reinstate herself through grief; she sheltered behind her bereavement, affecting a more profound seclusion, abhorring strangers; she was more than ever the reserved, fastidious daughter of Hilton Frean. She had always thought of herself as different from Connie and Sarah, living with a superior, intellectual life. She turned to the books she had read with her mother, Dante, Browning, Carlyle, and Ruskin, the biographies of Great Men, trying to retrace the footsteps of her lost self, to revive the forgotten thrill. But it was no use. One day she found herself reading the Dedication of *The Ring and the Book* over and over again, without taking in its meaning, without any remembrance of its poignant secret. " 'And all a wonder and a wild desire'—Mamma loved that." She thought she loved it too; but what she loved was the dark-green book she had seen in her mother's long, white hands, and the sound of her mother's voice reading. She had followed her mother's mind with strained attention and anxiety, smiling when she smiled, but with no delight and no admiration of her own.

If only she could have remembered. It was only through memory that she could reinstate herself.

She had a horror of the empty house. Her friends advised her to leave it, but she had a horror of removal, of change. She loved the rooms that had held her mother, the chair she had sat on, the white, fluted cup she had drunk from in her illness. She clung to the image of her mother; and always beside it, shadowy and pathetic, she discerned the image of her lost self.

When the horror of emptiness came over her, she dressed herself in her black, with delicate care and precision, and visited her friends. Even in moments of no intention she would find herself knocking at Lizzie's door or Sarah's or Connie Pennefather's. If they were not in she would call again and again, till she found them. She would sit for hours, talking, spinning out the time.

She began to look forward to these visits.

Wonderful. The sweet peas she had planted had come up.

Hitherto Harriett had looked on the house and garden as parts of the space that contained her without belonging to her. She had had no sense of possession. This morning she was arrested by the thought that the plot she had planted was hers. The house and garden were hers. She began to take an interest in them. She found that by a system of punctual movements she could give to her existence the reasonable appearance of an aim.

Next spring, a year after her mother's death, she felt the vague stirring of her individual soul. She was free to choose her own vicar; she left her mother's Dr. Braithwaite, who was broad and twice married, and went to Canon Wrench, who was unmarried and high. There was something stimulating in the short, happy service, the rich music, the incense, and the processions. She made new covers for the drawing-room, in cretonne, a gay pattern of pomegranate and blue-green leaves. And as she had always had the cutlets broiled plain because her mother liked them that way, now she had them breaded.

And Mrs. Hancock wanted to know *why* Harriett had forsaken her dear mother's church; and when Connie Pennefather saw the covers she told Harriett she was lucky to be able to afford new cretonne. It was more than *she* could; she seemed to think Harriett had no business to afford it. As for the breaded cutlets, Hannah opened her eyes and said, "That was how the mistress always had them, ma'am, when you was away."

One day she took the blue egg out of the drawing-room and stuck it on the chimney-piece in the spare room. When she remembered how she used to love it she felt that she had done something cruel and iniquitous, but necessary to the soul.

She was taking out novels from the circulating library now. Not, she explained, for her serious reading. Her serious reading, her Dante, her Browning, her Great Man, lay always on the table ready to her hand (beside a copy of *The Social Order* and the *Remains* of Hilton Frean) while secretly and half-ashamed she played with some frivolous tale. She was satisfied with anything that ended happily and had nothing in it that was unpleasant, or difficult, demanding thought. She exalted her preferences into high canons. A novel *ought* to conform to her requirements. A novelist (she thought of him with some asperity) had no right to be obscure, or depressing, or to add needless unpleasantness to the unpleasantness that had to be. The Great Men didn't *do* it.

She spoke of George Eliot and Dickens and Mr. Thackeray.

Lizzie Pierce had a provoking way of smiling at Harriett, as if she found her ridiculous. And Harriett had no patience with Lizzie's affectation in wanting to be modern, her vanity in trying to be young, her middle-aged raptures over the work—often unpleasant—of writers too young to be worth serious consideration. They had long arguments in which Harriett, beaten, retired behind *The Social Order* and the *Remains*.

"It's silly," Lizzie said, "not to be able to look at a new thing because it's new. That's the way you grow old."

"It's sillier," Harriett said, "to be always running after new things because you think that's the way to look young. I've no wish to appear younger than I am."

"I've no wish to appear suffering from senile decay."

"There *is* a standard." Harriett lifted her obstinate and arrogant chin. "You forget that I'm Hilton Frean's daughter."

"I'm William Pierce's, but that hasn't prevented my being myself."

Lizzie's mind had grown keener in her sharp middle age. As it played about her, Harriett cowered; it was like being exposed, naked, to a cutting wind. Her mind ran back to her father and mother, longing, like a child, for their shelter and support, for the blessed assurance of herself.

At her worst she could still think with pleasure of the beauty of the act which had given Robin to Priscilla.

X

"My dear Harriett: Thank you for your kind letter of sympathy. Although we had expected the end for many weeks poor Prissie's death came to us as a great shock. But for her it was a blessed release, and we can only be thankful. You who knew her will realize the depth and extent of my bereavement. I have lost the dearest and most loving wife man ever had. . . ."

Poor little Prissie. She couldn't bear to think she would never see her again.

Six months later Robin wrote again, from Sidmouth.

"Dear Harriett: Priscilla left you this locket in her will as a re-membrance. I would have sent it before but that I couldn't bear to part with her things all at once.

"I take this opportunity of telling you that I am going to be married again———"

Her heart heaved and closed. She could never have believed she could have felt such a pang.

"The lady is Miss Beatrice Walker, the devoted nurse who was with my dear wife all through her last illness. This step may seem strange and precipitate, coming so soon after her death; but I am urged to do it by the precarious state of my own health and by the knowledge that we are fulfilling poor Prissie's dying wish...."

Poor Prissie's dying wish. After what she had done for Prissie, if she *had* a dying wish——But neither of them had thought of her. Robin had forgotten her.... Forgotten.... Forgotten.

But no. Priscilla had remembered. She had left her the locket with his hair in it. She had remembered and she had been afraid; jealous of her. She couldn't bear to think that Robin might marry her, even after she was dead. She had made him marry this Walker woman so that he shouldn't——

Oh, but he wouldn't. Not after twenty years.

"I didn't really think he would."

She was forty-five, her face was lined and pitted and her hair was dust color, streaked with gray: and she could only think of Robin as she had last seen him, young: a young face; a young body; young, shining eyes. He would want to marry a young woman. He had been in love with this Walker woman, and Prissie had known it. She could see Prissie lying in her bed, helpless, looking at them over the edge of the white sheet. She had known that as soon as she was dead, before the sods closed over her grave, they would marry. Nothing could stop them. And she had tried to make herself believe it was her wish, her doing, not theirs. Poor little Prissie.

She understood that Robin had been staying in Sidmouth for his health.

A year later, Harriett, run down, was ordered to the seaside. She went to Sidmouth. She told herself that she wanted to see the place where she had been so happy with her mother, where poor Aunt Harriett had died.

Looking through the local paper she found in the list of residents: Sidcote—Mr. and Mrs. Robert Lethbridge and Miss Walker. She wrote to Robin and asked if she might call on his wife.

A mile of hot road through the town and inland brought her to a door in a lane and a thatched cottage with a little lawn behind it. From the door-step she could see two figures, a man and a woman, lying back in garden chairs. Inside the house she heard the persistent, energetic sound of hammering. The woman got up and came to her. She was young, pink-faced and golden-haired, and she said she was Miss Walker, Mrs. Lethbridge's sister.

A tall, lean, gray man rose from the garden chair, slowly, dragging himself with an invalid air. His eyes stared, groping, blurred films that trembled between the pouch and droop of the lids; long cheeks, deep grooved, dropped to the infirm mouth that sagged under the limp mustache. That was Robin.

He became agitated when he saw her. "Poor Robin," she thought. "All these years, and it's too much for him, seeing me." Presently he dragged himself from the lawn to the house and disappeared through the French window where the hammering came from.

"Have I frightened him away?" she said.

"Oh, no, he's always like that when he sees strange faces."

"My face isn't exactly strange."

"Well, he must have thought it was."

A sudden chill crept through her.

"He'll be all right when he gets used to you," Miss Walker said.

The strange face of Miss Walker chilled her. A strange young woman, living close to Robin, protecting him, explaining Robin's ways.

The sound of hammering ceased. Through the long, open

window she saw a woman rise up from the floor and shed a white apron. She came down the lawn to them, with raised arms, patting disordered hair; large, a full, firm figure clipped in blue linen. A full-blown face, bluish pink; thick gray eyes slightly protruding; a thick mouth, solid and firm and kind. That was Robin's wife. Her sister was slighter, fresher, a good ten years younger, Harriett thought.

"Excuse me, we're only just settling in. I was nailing down the carpet in Robin's study."

Her lips were so thick that they moved stiffly when she spoke or smiled. She panted a little as if from extreme exertion.

When they were all seated Mrs. Lethbridge addressed her sister. "Robin was quite right. It looks *much* better turned the other way."

"Do you mean to say he made you take it all up and put it down again? Well——"

"What's the use? . . . Miss Frean, you don't know what it is to have a husband who *will* have things just so."

"She had to mow the lawn this morning because Robin can't bear to see one blade of grass higher than another."

"Is he as particular as all that?"

"I assure you, Miss Frean, he is," Miss Walker informed her.

"He wasn't when I knew him," Harriett said.

"Ah—my sister spoils him."

Mrs. Lethbridge wondered why he hadn't come out again.

"I think," Harriett said, "perhaps he'll come if I go."

"Oh, you mustn't go. It's good for him to see people. Takes him out of himself."

"He'll turn up all right," Miss Walker said, "when he hears the teacups."

And at four o'clock when the teacups came, Robin turned up, dragging himself slowly from the house to the lawn. He blinked and quivered with agitation; Harriett saw he was annoyed, not with her, and not with Miss Walker, but with his wife.

"Beatrice, what have you done with my new bottle of medicine?"

"Nothing, dear."

"You've done nothing, when you know you poured out my last dose at twelve?"

"Why, hasn't it come?"

"No. It hasn't."

"But Cissy ordered it this morning."

"I didn't," Cissy said. "I forgot."

"Oh, Cissy——"

"You needn't blame Cissy. You ought to have seen to it yourself.... She was a good nurse, Harriett, before she was my wife."

"My dear, your nurse had nothing else to do. Your wife has to clean and mend for you, and cook your dinner and mow the lawn and nail the carpets down." While she said it she looked at Robin as if she adored him.

All through tea time he talked about his health and about the sanitary dustbin they hadn't got. Something had happened to him. It wasn't like him to be wrapped up in himself and to talk about dustbins. He spoke to his wife as if she had been his valet. He didn't see that she was perspiring, worn out by her struggle with the carpet.

"Just go and fetch me another cushion, Beatrice."

She rose with tired patience.

"You might let her have her tea in peace," Miss Walker said, but she was gone before they could stop her.

When Harriett left she went with her to the garden gate, panting as she walked. Harriett noticed pale, blurred lines on the edges of her lips. She thought: She isn't a bit strong. She praised the garden.

Mrs. Lethbridge smiled. "Robin loves it. . . . But you should have seen it at five o'clock this morning."

"Five o'clock?"

"Yes. I always get up at five to make Robin a cup of tea."

Harriett's last evening. She was dining at Sidcote. On her way there she had overtaken Robin's wife wheeling Robin in a bath chair. Beatrice had panted and perspired and had made mute signs to Harriett not to take any notice. She had had to go and lie down till Robin sent for her to find his cigarette case. Now she was in the kitchen cooking Robin's part of the dinner while he lay down in his study. Harriett talked to Miss Walker in the garden.

"It's been very kind of you to have us so much."

"Oh, but we've loved having you. It's so good for Beatie. Gives her a rest from Robin. . . . I don't mean that she wants a rest. But, you see, she's not well. She looks a big, strong, bouncing thing, but she isn't. Her heart's weak. She oughtn't to be doing what she does."

"Doesn't Robin see it?"

"He doesn't see anything. He never knows when she's tired or got a headache. She'll drop dead before he'll see it. He's utterly selfish, Miss Frean. Wrapt up in himself and his horrid little ailments. Whatever happens to Beatie he must have his sweetbread, and his soup at eleven and his tea at five in the morning. . . ."

". . . I suppose you think I might help more?"

"Well——" Harriett did think it.

"Well, I just won't. I won't encourage Robin. He ought to get her a proper servant and a man for the garden and the bath chair. I wish you'd give him a hint. Tell him she isn't strong. I can't. She'd snap my head off. Would you mind?"

Harriett didn't mind. She didn't mind what she said. She

wouldn't be saying it to Robin, but to the contemptible thing that had taken Robin's place. She still saw Robin as a young man, with young, shining eyes, who came rushing to give himself up at once, to make himself known. She had no affection for this selfish invalid, this weak, peevish bully.

Poor Beatrice. She was sorry for Beatrice. She resented his behavior to Beatrice. She told herself she wouldn't be Beatrice, she wouldn't be Robin's wife for the world. Her pity for Beatrice gave her a secret pleasure and satisfaction.

After dinner she sat out in the garden talking to Robin's wife, while Cissy Walker played draughts with Robin in his study, giving Beatrice a rest from him. They talked about Robin.

"You knew him when he was young, didn't you? What was he like?"

She didn't want to tell her. She wanted to keep the young, shining Robin to herself. She also wanted to show that she had known him, that she had known a Robin that Beatrice would never know. Therefore she told her.

"My poor Robin." Beatrice gazed wistfully, trying to see this Robin that Priscilla had taken from her, that Harriett had known. Then she turned her back.

"It doesn't matter. I've married the man I wanted." She let herself go. "Cissy says I've spoiled him. That isn't true. It was his first wife who spoiled him. She made a nervous wreck of him."

"He was devoted to her."

"Yes. And he's paying for his devotion now. She wore him out. . . . Cissy says he's selfish. If he is, it's because he's used up all his unselfishness. He was living on his moral capital. . . . I feel as if I couldn't do too much for him after what he did. Cissy doesn't know how awful his life was with Priscilla. She was the most exacting——"

"She was my friend."

"Wasn't Robin your friend, too?"

"Yes. But poor Prissie, she was paralyzed."

"It wasn't paralysis."

"What was it then?"

"Pure hysteria. Robin wasn't in love with her, and she knew it. She developed that illness so that she might have a hold on him, get his attention fastened on her somehow. I don't say she could help it. She couldn't. But that's what it was."

"Well, she died of it."

"No. She died of pneumonia after influenza. I'm not blaming Prissie. She was pitiable. But he ought never to have married her."

"I don't think you ought to say that."

"You know what he was," said Robin's wife. "And look at him now."

But Harriett's mind refused, obstinately, to connect the two Robins and Priscilla.

She remembered that she had to speak to Robin. They went together into his study. Cissy sent her a look, a signal, and rose; she stood by the doorway.

"Beatie, you might come here a minute."

Harriett was alone with Robin.

"Well, Harriett, we haven't been able to do much for you. In my beastly state——"

"You'll get better."

"Never. I'm done for, Harriett. I don't complain."

"You've got a devoted wife, Robin."

"Yes. Poor girl, she does what she can."

"She does too much."

"My dear woman, she wouldn't be happy if she didn't."

"It isn't good for her. Does it never strike you that she's not strong?"

"Not strong? She's—she's almost indecently robust. What wouldn't I give to have her strength!"

She looked at him, at the lean figure sunk in the armchair, at the dragged, infirm face, the blurred, owlish eyes, the expression of abject self-pity, of self-absorption.

That was Robin.

The awful thing was that she couldn't love him, couldn't go on being faithful. This injured her self-esteem.

XI

Her old servant, Hannah, had gone, and her new servant, Maggie, had had a baby.

After the first shock and three months' loss of Maggie, it occurred to Harriett that the beautiful thing would be to take Maggie back and let her have the baby with her, since she couldn't leave it.

The baby lay in his cradle in the kitchen, black-eyed and rosy, doubling up his fat, naked knees, smiling his crooked smile, and saying things to himself. Harriett had to see him every time she came into the kitchen. Sometimes she heard him cry, an intolerable cry, tearing the nerves and heart. And sometimes she saw Maggie unbutton her black gown in a hurry and put out her white, rose-pointed breast to still his cry.

Harriett couldn't bear it. She could not bear it.

She decided that Maggie must go. Maggie was not doing her work properly. Harriett found flue under the bed.

"I'm sure," Maggie said, "I'm doing no worse than I did, ma'am, and you usedn't to complain."

"No worse isn't good enough, Maggie. I think you might have tried to please me. It isn't every one who would have taken you in the circumstances."

"If you think that, ma'am, it's very cruel and unkind of you to send me away."

"You've only yourself to thank. There's no more to be said."

"No, ma'am. I understand why I'm leaving. It's because of Baby. You don't want to 'ave 'im, and I think you might have said so before."

That day month Maggie packed her brown-painted wooden box and the cradle and the perambulator. The greengrocer took them away on a handcart. Through the drawing-room window Harriett saw Maggie going away, carrying the baby, pink and round in his white-knitted cap, his fat hips bulging over her arm under his white shawl. The gate fell to behind them. The click struck at Harriett's heart.

Three months later Maggie turned up again in a black hat and gown for best, red-eyed and humble.

"I came to see, ma'am, whether you'd take me back, as I 'aven't got Baby now."

"You haven't got him?"

" 'E died, ma'am, last month. I'd put him with a woman in the country. She was highly recommended to me. Very highly recommended she was, and I paid her six shillings a week. But I think she must 'ave done something she shouldn't."

"Oh, Maggie, you don't mean she was cruel to him?"

"No, ma'am. She was very fond of him. Everybody was fond of Baby. But whether it was the food she gave him or what, 'e was that wasted you wouldn't have known him. You remember what he was like when he was here."

"I remember."

She remembered. She remembered. Fat and round in his white

shawl and knitted cap when Maggie carried him down the garden path.

"I should think she'd a done something, shouldn't you, ma'am?"

She thought: No. No. It was I who did it when I sent him away.

"I don't know, Maggie. I'm afraid it's been very terrible for you."

"Yes, ma'am. . . . I wondered whether you'd give me another trial, ma'am."

"Are you quite sure you want to come to me, Maggie?"

"Yes'm. . . . I'm sure you'd a kept him if you could have borne to see him about."

"You know, Maggie, that was *not* the reason why you left. If I take you back you must try not to be careless and forgetful."

"I shan't 'ave nothing to make me. Before, it was first Baby's father and then 'im."

She could see that Maggie didn't hold her responsible. After all, why should she? If Maggie had made bad arrangements for her baby, Maggie was responsible.

She went round to Lizzie and Sarah to see what they thought. Sarah thought: Well—it was rather a difficult question, and Harriett resented her hesitation.

"Not at all. It rested with Maggie to go or stay. If she was incompetent I wasn't bound to keep her just because she'd had a baby. At that rate I should have been completely in her power."

Lizzie said she thought Maggie's baby would have died in any case, and they both hoped that Harriett wasn't going to be morbid about it.

Harriett felt sustained. She wasn't going to be morbid. All the same, the episode left her with a feeling of insecurity.

XII

The young girl, Robin's niece, had come again, bright-eyed, eager, and hungry, grateful for Sunday supper.

Harriett was getting used to these appearances, spread over three years, since Robin's wife had asked her to be kind to Mona Floyd. Mona had come this time to tell her of her engagement to Geoffrey Carter. The news shocked Harriett intensely.

"But, my dear, you told me he was going to marry your little friend, Amy—Amy Lambert. What does Amy say to it?"

"What *can* she say? I know it's a bit rough on her——"

"You know; and yet you'll take your happiness at the poor child's expense."

"We've got to. We can't do anything else."

"Oh, my dear——" If she could stop it. . . . An inspiration came. "I knew a girl once who might have done what you're doing, only she wouldn't. She gave the man up rather than hurt her friend. She *couldn't do anything else.*"

"How much was he in love with her?"

"I don't know *how much*. He was never in love with any other woman."

"Then she was a fool. A silly fool. Didn't she think of *him?*"

"Didn't she think!"

"No. She didn't. She thought of herself. Of her own moral beauty. She was a selfish fool."

"She asked the best and wisest man she knew, and he told her she couldn't do anything else."

"The best and wisest man—oh, Lord!"

"That was my own father, Mona, Hilton Frean."

"Then it was you. You and Uncle Robin and Aunt Prissie."

Harriett's face smiled its straight, thin-lipped smile, the worn, grooved chin arrogantly lifted.

"How could you?"

"I could because I was brought up not to think of myself before other people."

"Then it wasn't even your own idea. You sacrificed him to somebody else's. You made three people miserable just for that. Four, if you count Aunt Beatie."

"There was Prissie. I did it for her."

"What did you do for her? You insulted Aunt Prissie."

"Insulted her? My dear Mona!"

"It was an insult, handing her over to a man who couldn't love her even with his body. Aunt Prissie was the miserablest of the lot. Do you suppose he didn't take it out of her?"

"He never let her know."

"Oh, didn't he! She knew all right. That's how she got her illness. And it's how he got his. And he'll kill Aunt Beatie. He's taking it out of *her* now. Look at the awful suffering. And you can go on sentimentalizing about it."

The young girl rose, flinging her scarf over her shoulders with a violent gesture.

"There's no common sense in it."

"No *common* sense, perhaps."

"It's a jolly sight better than sentiment when it comes to marrying."

They kissed. Mona turned at the doorway.

"I say—did he go on caring for you?"

"Sometimes I think he did. Sometimes I think he hated me."

"Of course he hated you, after what you'd let him in for." She paused. "You don't *mind* my telling you the truth, do you?"

. . . Harriett sat a long time, her hands folded on her lap, her eyes staring into the room, trying to see the truth. She saw the girl, Robin's niece, in her young indignation, her tender brilliance suddenly hard, suddenly cruel, flashing out the truth. Was it true that she had sacrificed Robin and Priscilla and Beatrice to her parents' idea of moral beauty? Was it true that this idea had been all wrong? That she might have married Robin and been happy and been right?

"I don't care. If it was to be done again to-morrow I'd do it."

But the beauty of that unique act no longer appeared to her as it once was, uplifting, consoling, incorruptible.

The years passed. They went with an incredible rapidity, and Harriett was now fifty.

The feeling of insecurity had grown on her. It had something to do with Mona, with Maggie and Maggie's baby. She had no clear illumination, only a mournful acquiescence in her own futility, an almost physical sense of shrinkage, the crumbling away, bit by bit, of her beautiful and honorable self, dying with the objects of its three profound affections: her father, her mother, Robin. Gradually the image of the middle-aged Robin had effaced his youth.

She read more and more novels from the circulating libraries, of a kind demanding less and less effort of attention. And always her inability to concentrate appeared to her as a just demand for clarity: "The man has no *business* to write so that I can't understand him."

She laid in a weekly stock of opinions from *The Spectator,* and by this means contrived a semblance of intellectual life.

She was appeased more and more by the rhythm of the seasons, of the weeks, of day and night, by the first coming up of the pink and wine-brown velvet primulas, by the pungent, burnt smell of her morning coffee, the smell of a midday stew, of hot cakes baking for tea time; by the lighting of the lamp, the lighting of autumn fires, the round of her visits. She waited with a strained, expectant desire for the moment when it would be time to see Lizzie or Sarah or Connie Pennefather again.

Seeing them was a habit she couldn't get over. But it no longer gave her keen pleasure. She told herself that her three friends were deteriorating in their middle age. Lizzie's sharp face darted malice; her tongue was whipcord; she knew where to flick; the small gleam of her eyes, the snap of her nutcracker jaws irritated Harriett. Sarah was slow; slow. She took no care of her face and figure. As Lizzie put it, Sarah's appearance was an outrage on her contemporaries. "She makes us feel so old."

And Connie—the very rucking of Connie's coat about her broad hips irritated Harriett. She had a way of staring over her fat cheeks at Harriett's old suits, mistaking them for new ones, and saying the same exasperating thing. "You're lucky to be able to afford it. *I* can't."

Harriett's irritation mounted up and up.

And one day she quarreled with Connie.

Connie had been telling one of her stories; leaning a little sideways, her skirt stretched tight between her fat, parted knees, the broad roll of her smile sliding greasily. She had "grown out of it" in her young womanhood, and now in her middle age she had come back to it again. She was just like her father.

"Connie, how can you be so coarse?"

"I beg pardon. I forgot you were always better than everybody else."

"I'm not better than everybody else. I've only been brought up better than some people. My father would have died rather than have told a story like that."

"I suppose that's a dig at my parents."

"I never said anything about your parents."

"I know the things you think about my father."

"Well—I daresay he thinks things about me."

"He thinks you were always an incurable old maid, my dear."

"Did he think my father was an old maid?"

"I never heard him say one unkind word about your father."

"I should hope not, indeed."

"Unkind things were said. Not by him. Though he might have been forgiven——"

"I don't know what you mean. But all my father's creditors were paid in full. You know that."

"I didn't know it."

"You know it now. Was your father one of them?"

"No. It was as bad for him as if he had been, though."

"How do you make that out?"

"Well, my dear, if he hadn't taken your father's advice he might have been a rich man now instead of a poor one. . . . He invested all his money as he told him."

"In my father's things?"

"In things he was interested in. And he lost it."

"It shows how he must have trusted him."

"He wasn't the only one who was ruined by his trust."

Harriett blinked. Her mind swerved from the blow. "I think you must be mistaken," she said.

"I'm less likely to be mistaken than you, my dear, though he *was* your father."

Harriett sat up, straight and stiff. "Well, *your* father's alive, and *he's* dead."

"I don't see what that has to do with it."

"Don't you? If it had happened the other way about, your father wouldn't have died."

Connie stared stupidly at Harriett, not taking it in. Presently she got up and left her. She moved clumsily, her broad hips shaking.

Harriett put on her hat and went round to Lizzie and Sarah in turn. They would know whether it were true or not. They would know whether Mr. Hancock had been ruined by his own fault or Papa's.

Sarah was sorry. She picked up a fold of her skirt and crumpled it in her fingers, and said over and over again, "She oughtn't to have told you." But she didn't say it wasn't true. Neither did Lizzie, though her tongue was a whip for Connie.

"Because you can't stand her dirty stories she goes and tells you this. It shows what Connie is."

It showed her father as he was, too. Not wise. Not wise all the time. Courageous, always, loving danger, intolerant of security, wild under all his quietness and gentleness, taking madder and madder risks, playing his game with an awful, cool recklessness. Then letting other people in; ruining Mr. Hancock, the little man he used to laugh at. And it had killed him. He hadn't been sorry for Mamma, because he knew she was glad the mad game was over; but he had thought and thought about him, the little dirty man, until he had died of thinking.

XIII

New people had come to the house next door. Harriett saw a pretty girl going in and out. She had not called; she was not going to call. Their cat came over the garden wall and bit off the blades of the irises. When he sat down on the mignonette Harriett sent a note round by Maggie: "Miss Frean presents her compliments to the lady next door and would be glad if she would restrain her cat."

Five minutes later the pretty girl appeared with the cat in her arms.

"I've brought Mimi," she said. "I want you to see what a darling he is."

Mimi, a Persian, all orange on the top and snow white underneath, climbed her breast to hang flattened out against her shoulder, long, the great plume of his tail fanning her. She swung round to show the innocence of his amber eyes and the pink arch of his mouth supporting his pink nose.

"I want *you* to see my mignonette," said Harriett. They stood together by the crushed ring where Mimi had made his bed.

The pretty girl said she was sorry. "But, you see, we *can't* restrain him. I don't know what's to be done. . . . Unless you kept a cat yourself; then you won't mind."

"But," Harriett said, "I don't like cats."

"Oh, *why* not?"

Harriett knew why. A cat was a compromise, a substitute, a subterfuge. Her pride couldn't stoop. She was afraid of Mimi, of his enchanting play, and the soft white fur of his stomach. Maggie's baby. So she said, "Because they destroy the beds. And they kill birds."

The pretty girl's chin burrowed in Mimi's neck. "You *won't* throw stones at him?" she said.

"No, I wouldn't *hurt* him. . . . What did you say his name was?"

"Mimi."

Harriett softened. She remembered. "When I was a little girl I had a cat called Mimi. White Angora. Very handsome. And your name is——"

"Brailsford. I'm Dorothy."

Next time, when Mimi jumped on the lupins and broke them down, Dorothy came again and said she was sorry. And she stayed to tea. Harriett revealed herself.

"My father was Hilton Frean." She had noticed for the last fifteen years that people showed no interest when she told them that. They even stared as though she had said something that had no sense in it. Dorothy said, "How nice."

"Nice?"

"I mean it must have been nice to have him for your father. . . . You don't mind my coming into your garden last thing to catch Mimi?"

Harriett felt a sudden yearning for Dorothy. She saw a pleasure, a happiness, in her coming. She wasn't going to call, but she sent little notes in to Dorothy asking her to come to tea.

Dorothy declined.

But every evening, towards bedtime, she came into the garden to catch Mimi. Through the window Harriett could hear her calling: "Mimi! Mimi!" She could see her in her white frock, moving about, hovering, ready to pounce as Mimi dashed from the bushes. She thought: "She walks into my garden as if it was her own. But she won't make a friend of me. She's young, and I'm old."

She had a piece of wire netting put up along the wall to keep Mimi out.

"That's the end of it," she said. She could never think of the young girl without a pang of sadness and resentment.

Fifty-five. Sixty.

In her sixty-second year Harriett had her first bad illness.

It was so like Sarah Barmby. Sarah got influenza and regarded it as a common cold and gave it to Harriett who regarded it as a common cold and got pleurisy.

When the pain was over she enjoyed her illness, the peace and rest of lying there, supported by the bed, holding out her lean arms to be washed by Maggie; closing her eyes in bliss while Maggie combed and brushed and plaited her fine gray hair. She liked having the same food at the same hours. She would look up, smiling weakly, when Maggie came at bedtime with the little tray. "What have you brought me *now*, Maggie?"

"Benger's Food, ma'am."

She wanted it to be always Benger's Food at bedtime. She lived by habit, by the punctual fulfillment of her expectation. She loved the doctor's visits at twelve o'clock, his air of brooding absorption in her case, his consultations with Maggie, the seriousness and sanctity he attached to the humblest details of her existence.

Above all she loved the comfort and protection of Maggie, the sight of Maggie's broad, tender face as it bent over her, the feeling of Maggie's strong arms as they supported her, the hovering pressure of the firm, broad body in the clean white apron and the cap. Her eyes rested on it with affection; she found shelter in Maggie as she had found it in her mother.

One day she said, "Why did you come to me, Maggie? Couldn't you have found a better place?"

"There was many wanted me. But I came to you, ma'am, because you seemed to sort of need me most. I dearly love looking after people. Old ladies and children. And gentlemen, if they're ill enough," Maggie said.

"You're a good girl, Maggie."

She had forgotten. The image of Maggie's baby was dead, hidden, buried deep down in her mind. She closed her eyes. Her head was thrown back, motionless, ecstatic under Maggie's flickering fingers as they plaited her thin wisps of hair.

Out of the peace of illness she entered on the misery and long labor of convalescence. The first time Maggie left her to dress herself she wept. She didn't want to get well. She could see nothing in recovery but the end of privilege and prestige, the obligation to return to a task she was tired of, a difficult and terrifying task.

By summer she was up and (tremulously) about again.

XIV

She was aware of her drowsy, supine dependence on Maggie. At first her perishing self asserted itself in an increased reserve and arrogance. Thus she protected herself from her own censure. She had still a feeling of satisfaction in her exclusiveness, her power not to call on new people.

"I think," Lizzie Pierce said, "you might have called on the Brailsfords."

"Why should I? I should have nothing in common with such people."

"Well, considering that Mr. Brailsford writes in *The Spectator*——"

Harriett called. She put on her gray silk and her soft white mohair shawl, and her wide black hat tied under her chin, and called. It was on a Saturday. The Brailsfords' room was full of visitors, men and women, talking excitedly. Dorothy was not there—Dorothy was married. Mimi was not there—Mimi was dead.

Harriett made her way between the chairs, dim-eyed, upright, and stiff in her white shawl. She apologized for having waited seven years before calling. . . . "Never go anywhere. . . . Quite a recluse since my father's death. He was Hilton Frean."

"Yes?" Mrs. Brailsford's eyes were sweetly interrogative.

"But as we are such near neighbors I felt that I must break my rule."

Mrs. Brailsford smiled in vague benevolence; yet as if she thought that Miss Frean's feeling and her action were unnecessary. After seven years. And presently Harriett found herself alone in her corner.

She tried to talk to Mr. Brailsford when he handed her the tea and bread and butter. "My father," she said, "was connected with *The Spectator* for many years. He was Hilton Frean."

"Indeed? I'm afraid I—don't remember."

She could get nothing out of him, out of his lean, ironical face, his eyes screwed up behind his glasses, benevolent, amused at her. She was nobody in that roomful of keen, intellectual people; nobody; nothing but an unnecessary little old lady who had come there uninvited.

Her second call was not returned. She heard that the Brailsfords were exclusive; they wouldn't know anybody out of their own set. Harriett explained her position thus: "No. I didn't keep it up. We have nothing in common."

She was old—old. She had nothing in common with youth, nothing in common with middle age, with intellectual, exclusive people connected with *The Spectator*. She said, *"The Spectator* is not what it used to be in my father's time."

Harriett Frean was not what she used to be. She was aware of the creeping fret, the poisons and obstructions of decay. It was as if she had parted with her own light, elastic body, and succeeded to somebody else's that was all bone, heavy, stiff, irresponsive to her

will. Her brain felt swollen and brittle, she had a feeling of tired-
ness in her face, of infirmity about her mouth. Her looking-glass
showed her the fallen yellow skin, the furrowed lines of age.

Her head dropped, drowsy, giddy over the week's accounts.
She gave up even the semblance of her housekeeping, and became permanently dependent on Maggie. She was happy in the
surrender of her responsibility, of the grown-up self she had
maintained with so much effort, clinging to Maggie, submitting
to Maggie, as she had clung and submitted to her mother.

Her affection concentrated on two objects, the house and
Maggie, Maggie and the house. The house had become a part of
herself, an extension of her body, a protective shell. She was un-
easy when away from it. The thought of it drew her with passion:
the low brown wall with the railing, the flagged path from the little green gate to the front door. The square brown front; the two
oblong, white-framed windows, the dark-green trellis porch between; the three windows above. And the clipped privet bush by
the trellis and the may tree by the gate.

She no longer enjoyed visiting her friends. She set out in peevish resignation, leaving her house, and when she had sat half an
hour with Lizzie or Sarah or Connie she would begin to fidget,
miserable till she got back to it again; to the house and Maggie.

She was glad enough when Lizzie came to her; she still liked
Lizzie best. They would sit together, one on each side of the fireplace, talking. Harriett's voice came thinly through her thin lips,
precise yet plaintive, Lizzie's finished with a snap of the bent-in
jaws.

"Do you remember those little round hats we used to wear?
You had one exactly like mine. Connie couldn't wear them."

"We were wild young things," said Lizzie.

"I was wilder than you. . . . A little audacious thing."

"And look at us now—we couldn't say 'Bo' to a goose. . . . Well, we may be thankful we haven't gone stout like Connie Pennefather."

"Or poor Sarah. That stoop."

They drew themselves up. Their straight, slender shoulders rebuked Connie's obesity, and Sarah's bent back, her bodice stretched hump-wise from the stuck-out ridges of her stays.

Harriett was glad when Lizzie went and left her to Maggie and the house. She always hoped she wouldn't stay for tea, so that Maggie might not have an extra cup and plate to wash.

The years passed: the sixty-third, sixty-fourth, sixty-fifth; their monotony mitigated by long spells of torpor and the sheer rapidity of time. Her mind was carried on, empty, in empty, flying time. She had a feeling of dryness and distension in all her being, and a sort of crepitation in her brain, irritating her to yawning fits. After meals, sitting in her armchair, her book would drop from her hands and her mind would slip from drowsiness into stupor. There was something voluptuous about the beginning of this state; she would give herself up to it with an animal pleasure and content.

Sometimes, for long periods, her mind would go backwards, returning, always returning, to the house in Black's Lane. She would see the row of elms and the white wall at the end with the green balcony hung out like a birdcage above the green door. She would see herself, a girl wearing a big chignon and a little round hat; or sitting in the curly chair with her feet on the white rug; and her father, slender and straight, smiling half-amused, while her mother read aloud to them. Or she was a child in a black silk apron going up Black's Lane. Little audacious thing. She had a fondness and admiration for this child and her audacity. And always she saw her mother, with her sweet face between the long, hanging curls, coming down the garden path, in a wide silver-gray gown trimmed with narrow bands of black velvet.

And she would wake up, surprised to find herself sitting in a strange room, dressed in a gown with strange sleeves that ended in old wrinkled hands; for the book that lay in her lap was Longfellow, open at *Evangeline*.

One day she made Maggie pull off the old, washed-out cretonne covers, exposing the faded blue rep. She was back in the drawing-room of her youth. Only one thing was missing. She went upstairs and took the blue egg out of the spare room and set it in its place on the marble-topped table. She sat gazing at it a long time in happy, child-like satisfaction. The blue egg gave reality to her return.

When she saw Maggie coming in with the tea and buttered scones she thought of her mother.

Three more years. Harriett was sixty-eight.

She had a faint recollection of having given Maggie notice, long ago, there, in the dining room. Maggie had stood on the hearthrug, in her large white apron, crying. She was crying now.

She said she must leave and go and take care of her mother. "Mother's getting very feeble now."

"I'm getting very feeble, too, Maggie. It's cruel and unkind of you to leave me."

"I'm sorry, ma'am. I can't help it."

She moved about the room, sniffing and sobbing as she dusted. Harriett couldn't bear it any more. "If you can't control yourself," she said, "go into the kitchen." Maggie went.

Harriett sat before the fire in her chair, straight and stiff, making no sound. Now and then her eyelids shook, fluttered red rims; slow, scanty tears oozed and fell, their trail glistening in the long furrows of her cheeks.

XV

The door of the specialist's house had shut behind them with a soft, respectful click.

Lizzie Pierce and Harriett sat in the taxicab, holding each other's hands. Harriett spoke.

"He says I've got what Mamma had."

Lizzie blinked away her tears; her hand loosened and tightened on Harriett's with a nervous clutch.

Harriett felt nothing but a strange, solemn excitement and exaltation. She was raised to her mother's eminence in pain. With every stab she would live again in her mother. She had what her mother had.

Only she would have an operation. This different thing was what she dreaded, the thing her mother hadn't had, and the going away into the hospital, to live exposed in the free ward among other people. That was what she minded most. That and leaving her house, and Maggie's leaving.

She cried when she saw Maggie standing at the gate in her white apron as the taxicab took her away. She thought, "When I come back again she won't be there." Yet somehow she felt that it wouldn't happen; it was impossible that she should come back and not find Maggie there.

She lay in her white bed in the white-curtained cubicle. Lizzie was paying for the cubicle. Kind Lizzie. Kind. Kind.

She wasn't afraid of the operation. It would happen in the morning. Only one thing worried her. Something Connie had told her. Under the anæsthetic you said things. Shocking, indecent things. But there wasn't anything she could say. She didn't know anything. . . . Yes. She did. There were Connie's stories. And Black's Lane. Behind the dirty blue palings in Black's Lane.

The nurses comforted her. They said if you kept your mouth tight shut, up to the last minute before the operation, if you didn't say one word you were all right.

She thought about it after she woke in the morning. For a whole hour before the operation she refused to speak, nodding and shaking her head, communicating by gestures. She walked down the wide corridor of the ward on her way to the theatre, very upright in her white flannel dressing gown, with her chin held high and a look of exaltation on her face. There were convalescents in the corridor. They saw her. The curtains before some of the cubicles were parted; the patients saw her; they knew what she was going to. Her exaltation mounted.

She came into the theatre. It was all white. White. White tiles. Rows of little slender knives on a glass shelf, under glass, shining. A white sink in the corner. A mixed smell of iodine and ether. The surgeon wore a white coat. Harriett made her tight lips tighter.

She climbed on to the white enamel table, and lay down, drawing her dressing gown straight about her knees. She had not said one word.

     •   •   •   •   •   •   •

She had behaved beautifully.

. . .

The pain in her body came up, wave after wave, burning. It swelled, tightening, stretching out her wounded flesh.

She knew that the little man they called the doctor was really Mr. Hancock. They oughtn't to have let him in. She cried out. "Take him away. Don't let him touch me;" but nobody took any notice.

"It isn't right," she said. "He oughtn't to do it. Not to *any* woman. If it was known he would be punished."

And there was Maggie by the curtain, crying.

"That's Maggie. She's crying because she thinks I killed her baby."

The ice bag laid across her body stirred like a live thing as the ice melted, then it settled and was still. She put her hand down and felt the smooth, cold oilskin distended with water.

"There's a dead baby in the bed. Red hair. They ought to have taken it away," she said. "Maggie had a baby once. She took it up the lane to the place where the man is; and they put it behind the palings. Dirty blue palings.

". . . Pussycat. Pussycat, what did you there? Pussy. Prissie. Prissiecat. Poor Prissie. She never goes to bed. She can't get up out of the chair."

A figure in white, with a stiff white cap, stood by the bed. She named it, fixed it in her mind. Nurse. Nurse—that was what it was. She spoke to it. "It's sad—sad to go through so much pain and then to have a dead baby."

The white curtain walls of the cubicle contracted, closed in on her. She was lying at the bottom of her white-curtained nursery cot. She felt weak and diminished, small, like a very little child.

The front curtains parted, showing the blond light of the corridor beyond. She saw the nursery door open and the light from the candle moved across the ceiling. The gap was filled by the heavy form, the obscene yet sorrowful face of Connie Pennefather.

Harriett looked at it. She smiled with a sudden ecstatic wonder and recognition.

"Mamma——"

READING GROUP GUIDE

1. May Sinclair has been credited with coining the phrase "stream-of-consciousness writing." How effective is her use of this technique in *Life and Death of Harriett Frean*?

2. In her Introduction, Francine Prose writes about "the oppressive weight and strength of the chains of family love, of the craving for parental approval." The example she cites is Mr. Frean's discussion with Harriett after her forbidden expedition down Black's Lane. Can you find other examples? What happens to young Harriett's rebellious streak?

3. Harriett devotes her life to "behaving beautifully." Which characters in the novel would agree that she had achieved this goal, and which would disagree? Do you think she "behaved beautifully"?

4. The critic Judy Cooke has described this book as "a disturbing analysis of English class and character." How does Harriett see her own social status in relation to her friends and her servant, Maggie? What happens to the social standing of the Frean family over the course of the novel?

5. The blue egg and red campion are two recurring images throughout the novel. What do you think they symbolize?

6. A year after her mother's death, Harriett feels "the vague stirring of her individual soul." What changes does she decide to make? Does she take full advantage of this new opportunity to make her own life choices?

7. According to the scholar Jean Radford, "the new science of psychoanalysis offered [Sinclair] a theory of mental functioning and she drew in particular on the Freudian notions of repression and sublimation." Can you find evidence of this in *Life and Death of Harriett Frean*? Consider the characters of Priscilla and Robin, as well as the Freans.

8. Prose writes, "It would be a mistake to assume that lives and deaths like Harriett Frean's ended with the Victorian era or that some modern version of Harriett's life isn't being lived at this very moment." Do you agree?

A NOTE ON THE TYPE

The principal text of this Modern Library edition
was set in a digitized version of Janson, a typeface that
dates from about 1690 and was cut by Nicholas Kis,
a Hungarian working in Amsterdam. The original matrices have
survived and are held by the Stempel foundry in Germany.
Hermann Zapf redesigned some of the weights and sizes for
Stempel, basing his revisions on the original design.

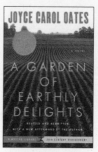